PRAISE

"Davis' writing de~~~ ~~ ~~~~~~~~~~~~~~~~ arp whit and satire against a well crafted sci-fi world. If you're a fan of *Black Mirror* then this book is for you."
ADAM PEARSON, BBC ACTOR AND TV PRESENTER. STAR OF THE OSCAR-NOMINATED *A DIFFERENT MAN* (2024)

"*HearRational* is a magic bullet right to the heart of conspiracy theories and how those on the fringes of belief are fed upon by the vampiric world of likes, clicks and views. Don't let the bastards drain you, read this blisteringly funny and expertly observed debut now!"
LAURIE BLAKE, STAR OF *NO ROLLS BARRED* AND *CHAOTIC NEUTRAL*

"With *HearRational*, Oli Davis shows that our terrifying world today is not beyond satire: doing for our century what Swift did for his. Davis' targets of the manosphere, academia, conspiracy theories, late-night talk shows and podcasts place us firmly in the catastrophe of now. There is no remedy finer than laughter through each sardonically dripped page. But for all its humour, *HearRational* is ultimately about communication and how in spite of love our grief has nowhere to go: an idea beyond satire."
CHRIS SIMPSON, PUSHCART PRIZE NOMINATED AUTHOR

"Davis has crafted a brilliantly clever and highly original world that will have you laughing as much as guessing what will come next."
LUKE OWEN, WRESTLETALK PRESENTER & AUTHOR OF *LIGHTS, CAMERA, GAME OVER!*

"A hilarious romp through a crazy world of interdimensional vampires, deranged conspiracy theories and bone telephones to the afterlife, only slightly less mad than our own!"
DOMINIC ALLEN, STAR OF *NO ROLLS BARRED*, *CHAOTIC NEUTRAL* AND *THE APOCALYPSE PLAYERS*

ABOUT THE AUTHOR

Oliver Davis has over 1 million subscribers to his various YouTube channels and podcasts, where he mostly talks about professional wrestling because it's less fake than real life (you can watch him at WrestleTalk). He has a First in both BA and MA Film Studies, and writes satirical science fiction. He lives in London with his cat, Kiki.

olidavis.com

OLIVER DAVIS

HearRational

www.vineleavespress.com

HearRational
Copyright © 2025 Oliver Davis

Cover design by Jessica Bell
Interior design by Amie McCracken

For Christine & Eric
(Nanny & Grandad)

SOMEWHERE
IN THE MIDDLE

Theo Papadopoulos was fifteen going on eternal. He had the serene smile and shaved head of Buddha. His wide, innocent eyes touched your very soul, if you believed in that kind of thing.

He hadn't been on Audrey's dinner party guest list.

She watched him dizzily across the living room. It was a shame, she thought, that he only spoke complete bollocks.

"Vampires are real," he said to a middle-aged man whose teeth were purple with wine. Audrey sipped at her fourth glass of Rioja and accidentally clunked the rim hard into her teeth. Or maybe it was drink number five.

"Don't be ridiculous, boy. Of course they aren't," replied Terrance Kettering, editor in chief of the *Royal Scientific* journal. His wine glass balanced on the shelf of his stomach. He would joke that his brain was in his belly, which was why it was so large. It took the sting out of being medically diagnosed as morbidly obese with type 2 diabetes.

"Maybe not in this dimension." Theo nodded. He was a rationally irrational boy.

Terrance sucked his violet lips. He pondered how best to explain the way objective truth really worked.

"We can't exactly prove that vampires *aren't* real. But there is also zero scientific evidence to prove they do exist either." He paused in thought. "It's like me telling you there's a wonderful palm tree on the ninth moon of Saturn. Possible? I suppose so. Likely? Not one bit. Some things are just easier to dismiss as nonsense." He grinned. "The fantasies of a defective mind, so to speak."

Audrey's boyfriend, Stephen, sniggered. She felt sick. If Theo was rationally irrational, the academics were stupidly smart. They didn't entertain an idea if it didn't fit with their beliefs.

Not that it mattered to Theo. His brain worked differently from everyone else's. Audrey had proved it, and that was about to make her famous.

Theo rubbed his shaved head and sighed. "They'll drain us all when they get here, unfortunately."

"When *who* gets here?" asked Stephen sharply.

"The vampires."

The other guests fell silent. Terrance stroked his belly-brain in thought. Audrey ignored Stephen's accusing stare.

"But don't worry," he reassured. "Audrey and I are going to save you all."

The room exploded with laughter.

Terrance raised his glass with one hand, held his belly with the other. "I thank you both in advance." He chuckled. He downed his wine. "This calls for another bottle, Stephen! We're going to be invaded by vampires! Drink the red stuff, friends. Drink the red stuff down, down, down!"

Audrey remembered a quote she'd once read about the problem with the world. *The smart people are full of doubts, while the stupid ones are full of confidence.* She weighed up her guests. In Terrance's case, that was pretty heavy. She couldn't say for sure which side was which.

She stumbled over to Stephen.

"I can't believe it." He snickered, topping up glasses. "He actually thinks vampires are real!"

Audrey gripped his wrist, half to steady herself, half to pull him down with her.

"Maybe they are," she spat. "Or maybe you just haven't found the right thing to drain you yet."

This is the story of how Audrey and Theo swindled a world.

CHAPTER 1: HERE COMES YOUR MAN: LIFE DECISIONS AS INFLUENCED BY MALE FIGURES

THEN

One year before the dinner party, Theo had become the only person in history, real or vampire, to be officially diagnosed with aural dyslexia. This was Audrey Lowe's greatest mistake. Her career never recovered.

Her hypothesis was that fringe and conspiracy beliefs weren't caused by social circumstances and mental conditions, as was widely accepted, but by physical trauma suffered to the brain. She developed this theory during her final years of postgraduate study, out of spite.

Developing grand, world-changing theories is ninety-seven percent staring out windows. Albert Einstein devised general relativity while bored at the Patent Office. Alexander Fleming discovered penicillin by forgetting about it on holiday. Isaac Newton formulated gravitational theory with a nap under an apple tree. So, to find inspiration for her PhD, and to earn money to buy books and eat (in that order), Audrey took the most mind-numbingly dull job she could find: working as a researcher for Dr. Samuel Worthington in the Psychology department at Canterbury University.

Dr. Samuel Worthington had built a moderately successful career on gaming the pop psychology system. His formula was devastatingly simple. Begin with the best clickbait headline, then reverse engineer a paper to fit it.

"You've got to do the journalists' work for them," he'd tell Audrey. "They're busy people who don't have time for the luxuries of richly detailed, double-blinded research papers. They need the facts. The most exciting facts."

Audrey slowly understood the heart-crushing truth. Journa*lism* was an ideal. Journa*lists* (focus on the *lists* because *10 AMAZING Facts You Didn't Know* … formats were their preferred way to tackle all topics) were people. Flawed, short-term thinking people, who had deadlines and page view targets and high-functioning Adderall habits. Journalists didn't have time for the *boring* facts. They only had time for titles.

"You've got to stand out in their electronic mails," Dr. Worthington told her. "Use the language they understand. Sell them on the clicks. Gift them the headline. *Pop* off the page!"

And to Dr. Worthington, there was no better pop psychology tabloid title than a play on the name of a popular song.

A brief index of Dr. Samuel Worthington's groundbreaking research:

"Girls Just Want to Have Fun … but Then Why Do Husbands Feel Nagged?"

"I'd Do Anything for Love (But I Won't … Open a Shared Bank Account): Why Couples Avoid Talking Money."

"Shiny Unhappy People: How the Life of the Party Is Actually a Manic Depressive."

After weeks of exhaustive research and tortured punning, Dr. Worthington had invented his latest perfectly publishable headline. He burst into their research lab one morning, marched purposefully to the whiteboard, the spring of solving Fermat's even-more-lost theorem in his step, and scrawled in six-inch-high, squeaky marker pen:

It's My Birthday, Do I Really Cry Because I Want To?

Dr. Worthington turned to the room. Only Audrey and two hungover undergraduate assistants were there. He crossed his arms and nodded with satisfaction, unaware the marker pen in his hand was leaving a grotesque, black blemish on the armpit of his shirt. It blotched and bruised, spreading across his chest and down his arm like a rapidly decaying necrosis.

"It's probably something about confronting one's own mortality," he offered helpfully. "And maybe a low-level fear of fire with the candles. Good luck!"

Audrey had to arrange and conduct interviews with the test subjects. She recruited a wide range of participants. Neuro-typical, neurodiverse, young children, adult children. As long as they were all asked the same standardized questions, the science would be pure.

Audrey considered herself very good at everything. The only thing she wasn't very good at was not being very good at everything. So even though she originally took the job to have more time to idly think, the study quickly consumed her life.

Not that there was much to consume.

She worked day and night, weekdays and weekends, through lunch breaks and family get-togethers. The mental tunneling was grueling, but she found grim contentment down the escapist rabbit hole of research. *Do I Really Cry Because I Want To?* was a riddle. She wanted to be the first to find the answer.

After one intense research stint of three days and eight Chinese takeaways, she found her Holy Grail (if she believed that kind of thing): a subject with early onset dementia, who woke up every day thinking it was their ninth birthday. The perfect controlled experiment.

The man was called Garry and, despite what he'd tell you, he was thirty-four years old. His hairline had retreated halfway up his head. His fingers were thick, hairy sausages. His elderly mother would shave his face every morning, old King Canute sweeping back an ageing tide in vain.

Audrey visited Garry twenty-two times in three months. She would always arrive promptly at 4:00 p.m., when a gray shadow was already casting itself across Garry's chin. The twenty-third time was her eureka.

"Happy birthday, Garry!" Audrey said, handing over his favorite, annoyingly discontinued, chocolate bar. She sat in an armchair veiled in a thin layer of dust. She pulled her sleeves as far over her hands as they'd reach so the decay couldn't touch her skin.

"Oh yum, Mum! A Marathon!" Garry said in his deep Liverpudlian accent.

"You get to eat it if you're a good boy and answer Dr. Lowe's questions."

Audrey wasn't a doctor. She didn't correct her.

Audrey began the same list of questions she'd asked Garry every time they met for the "first time."

"What day is it today?"

"It's my birthday! I turn nine today!"

Audrey avoided glancing at the dark hair on his forearms.

"That's wonderful news. But what day would that make it?"

"The thirteenth of April," Garry said, jiggling his man-sized fists in excitement.

Garry always answered *the thirteenth of April*. He had been wrong every time. Every time until now.

Audrey glanced at the calendar on the wall opposite. The thirteenth of April was circled in red permanent marker. She cross-referenced that against the date on her phone. *April 13.* Eventually, Garry's version of reality had lined up with everyone else's. Give or take twenty-five years.

Garry chomped down the Marathon bar and rested contently in its sugary aftereffects. Audrey watched him, the wrinkles of skin at the corner of his eyes, as his gaze floated up to the ceiling, lost in happy thoughts.

"Mum, will I get to do this again tomorrow?"

That was new. By his neurological definition, Garry didn't think about tomorrow.

"I'm afraid not, dear," his mother answered, trying to keep the surprise from her voice. "You only get one birthday a year."

Garry put a hand on his head. "So I'll turn nine again next year?"

"No, dear. You'll turn ten."

"But I don't want to be ten." Tears pooled in the corners of his eyes. His knee began to rattle. The chocolate bar wrapper crunched as Garry's hand clenched into a lonely, trembling fist. Audrey leaned forward. After a quarter of a century, he was finally snapping.

The experiment couldn't have been going any better.

"I want to be nine!"

"It's just the way the world works, dear. You'll get to love being loads of different ages, I promise."

"I don't want any different ages. I just want to be nine forever!"

Audrey checked her camera was recording. Tears streamed thick and heavy down Garry's bristled cheeks, which was excellent.

Garry suddenly turned to Audrey. "It's not my fault!" he shouted in a man's voice. He stood up. She jumped out of her chair, shaking dust into the airless room. It inhaled into her lungs as she gasped, itchy and drying down her throat. She backed away into the wall. Her elbow knocked something off the mantelpiece and it shattered on the marble base. A photo of twenty-something Garry and his parents lay on the carpet by her feet. Shards of glass covered them, a jigsaw that would never be complete. The door was blocked behind him. She had forgotten he was six foot three, two hundred and fifty pounds.

His mother stepped between them like a sheet of crate paper. "Garry, dear, it's okay—"

He pushed his mother to the floor. "The vampires are making me this way!" Garry cried. He stumbled toward Audrey on unsteady feet. "They're draining me." He grabbed hold of Audrey's arms. "Help me, please, Dr. Lowe. It's *draining* me."

Garry's father opened the living room door, holding a cake with nine candles.

"Happy birthday to you! Happy birthday to you! Happy birthday dear ..."

He saw his wife on the floor and his son holding their guest two inches off the ground. He sighed one continuous exhale, like he was a deflating birthday balloon.

"... Garry, what have you done?"

Garry's parents blamed themselves, like the best parents always should. Audrey accepted their apology and left immediately. Her arms throbbed where he had grabbed them. The skin on the back of her neck shivered. Her heart was full of trembling, awestruck ...

... glee!

She watched the footage back in the lab. Garry cried every day when he thought it was his birthday. But on his *actual* birthday, he cried seventeen percent more.

A stopped brain can be right once a year, even if it doesn't know why.

Audrey's boyfriend at the time was Stephen Pratt. He wouldn't shut up about a "cool idea" he wanted to contribute. He linked birthday crying to the original trauma of birth. He taught Comparative English Literature and Lacan's Other as Radical Counterpart of the Self, and said he knew a good story when he saw one.

Audrey told him if he knew a good story when he saw one, he should write one of his own like he always said he would.

"How am I going to prove that people unconsciously relive the trauma of birth on their birthday, Stephen?" she said. "Compare it to the feelings of people who were never born? Set up a little recording studio in utero? Interview babies fresh out the womb with a tiny microphone?"

He suggested starting with subjects born on leap years, which was annoying because Audrey was drunk when they were discussing this, and she couldn't figure out if that was a good solution.

Stephen Pratt was tall and lanky and Scottish. Audrey had once read a news article that said the Scottish accent was voted the most trustworthy in the nation. The poll had been conducted by Gosh! Bingo. They might just be a socially acceptable gateway to gambling for middle-aged women, but they were spot on about UK accents. Stephen's dialect was so thick she could swim in it.

They had met as undergraduates. Audrey had been enchanted by the sound of straight vowels and rolling r's drifting through her halls one night. That was what bagpipes should sound like, she thought. Mythical, romantic, strong. Not what they actually sounded like, which was two foxes fucking each other in a harpsichord.

She followed the *rrrrrr*'s down the fourth-floor corridor, up to the fifth and topmost level, and found Stephen sipping from a bag of wine perched on his shoulder. They bonded instantly over getting very, very drunk, staying up until the early hours of Tuesday mornings while scrawling naive manifestos for their respective disciplines. It was codependency at first sight.

Audrey was going to revolutionize the study of the mind. Her grandfather had vascular dementia, which was a degenerative mental condition caused by a stroke. She hoped to one day fix his mind by fixing his hardware, as if prodding a lobe or releasing a valve would help him tell Audrey, her mother, and his dead wife apart. She wanted to find the physical fixes for all mental health conditions. Then the days of psychiatry would be over. Humanity would enter the age of the physio for the mind.

Feeling sad?

We can massage your left frontal lobe to release happiness.

Feeling angry?

Your pituitary gland is inflamed, so take an ice bath to cool down.

You hate immigrants?

That's not your fault. It's because the part of your brain that deals with compassion isn't engaged enough. Your core muscles have become lazy because all you do is digest news gluten. Wear this electrostimulating vest. We can give you rock-hard empathy.

Audrey was going to fix society's brain.

Stephen, meanwhile, believed authors should only write from lived experience, in an idea he unironically referred to as otherness avoidance theory. The days of white, middle-class heterosexual males writing characters of black, gay, Hispanic, disabled, transgender, neurodiverse, or working-class perspectives should be banished to the past. Stephen declared white, middle-class, heterosexual males should only write white, middle-class, heterosexual male characters.

Audrey asked, what did he think Hollywood had been doing for the last century?

Once, in a minute of mental clarity, after she had finished her second bottle of red wine, and just before she was about to start a third, she had a moment of realization. Stephen's theory was to justify how, really, he had no imagination. She buried that thought deep down, because she loved him, refusing to soberly recognize how, from that moment on, she pitied him.

Audrey and Stephen would marry. She kept her maiden name for professional purposes, but, secretly, she would legally be Mrs. Pratt.

Dr. Worthington published "It's My Birthday, Do I Really Cry Because I Want To?" Audrey read it for the first time on *Psychology Tomorrow*'s website:

In summary, I, Dr. Samuel Worthington, have found a mixture of socioeconomic, evolutionary, and psychological causes of why young children and adult children are statistically more likely to cry on their own birthdays. But the most likely is the confrontation of one's own mortality, and a low-level fear of candle fire.

It was half baked, superficial, and ridden with conjecture. And worst, he hadn't put in a single mention of Audrey's study of Garry. His conclusion was just what he had believed from the start.

Audrey scrolled down to revel in the negative comments.

There were none. It was a hit.

"Whether or not it's objectively true doesn't matter," he explained to her over coffee. "It's that you got people thinking about a question. It's that you got them reading your work!"

Dr. Worthington was a hack.

Audrey drew her own conclusions from the study: human brains are dumb.

Natural selection didn't refine consciousness into perfect, lean organs. Instead, it patched it up over millennia. Gave updates to some parts, forgot about others. Never once did evolution do a full system-wide update. The human race was still running off the same version-one operating system they launched with. Like three hundred songs in your pocket was ever enough.

Consequently, it had no idea how to process modern life. It had been built for classic questions, like: *Can I eat this berry? Can I reproduce with that bison? Will this dinosaur eat me?*

Dinosaurs weren't around at the same time as humans, Stephen would say. Audrey sarcastically applauded him pointing out the obvious.

Ultimately, the brain does the best it can. The human mind tries, in its own dumb way, to maintain balance.

You cry at the happy parts in rom-coms. You laugh when you find nudes on your husband's phone. You find a baby so cute you say you want to eat it.

Feeling emotions of overwhelming happiness? Here, have all the memories of every stupid thing you've ever done.

Audrey expressed this in a simple formula:

Anxiety = Feeling Fucked > Happy

And so it is with birthdays. The intensely happy experience of your nearest and dearest gathering just for you, even if you don't like them, for the sole reason that it's been x number of years since you arrived on this Earth, provokes the opposite emotional response to balance you out.

She ranted all this to Stephen, drowning the sorrows of science into the early hours of the following morning.

"He's a hack!" Audrey said. "He already had his conclusion. He didn't care about anything I found!"

"It's frustrating," Stephen agreed, sitting across from her on their living room floor. He topped up her wine. "I thought we were really onto something with my original trauma of birth theory."

Stephen wasn't listening to her.

Audrey stormed out into the night, a bottle sloshing in her swinging right arm. Dr. Samuel Worthington, journa*lists*, Stephen ... when people hear a good enough story, no matter how half baked or disconnected from reality it is, they cling to it with the unrelenting grip of intellectual rigor mortis.

It's draining me, Garry's voice echoed in her head.

Audrey absentmindedly held the spot on her arm where he had lifted her up. Garry believed vampires were draining him, she remembered. How's that for a wild story disconnected from reality?

There was a study in that. A real, actual, scientific study. She'd do science herself.

NOW

Theo stood before his most loyal newsletter subscribers in the Marksman pub. They all looked like him but distorted. Some impossibly fat, some impossibly thin. It was like staring into a hall of crazy mirrors. They would've been all men, too, if one of his followers hadn't brought his mum.

They were supposed to have the Roundhead Room in the back, but the pub manager, Colin, got a last-minute retirement drinks booking. Instead, Theo shifted awkwardly beside the main bar in front of his crowd of fourteen, the rest of the Marksman's regulars, and a replica rifle hanging above a faded portrait of King George IV.

He cleared his throat, swallowed. His mouth tasted of bitter breakfast tea. Theo had never spoken to an audience of real, live people before. He was well versed talking to username avatars, but standing here, in front of offline actual humans with eye contact, made his head feel itchy.

He ran his hand through his hair. It was straighter than the flat Earth and felt silky between his fingers, even though he never washed it. His hand stopped at the base of his neck and massaged his shoulder. His hair continued down, brushing his lower back.

It had been seven years since he shaved his head bald to take part in an experiment. Those months had given him the confidence and belief to be who he was today. He had let it grow long ever since as a promise. He would only get a haircut once he'd restored the good Dr. Audrey's name.

His audience, and a Jack Russell that had been lapping water beneath the bar, waited with anticipation. Or for someone to throw them a bone.

"Proof!" yelped Ian in encouragement, a middle-aged accountant sitting in the second row. Theo had been speaking to him online for five years, and they were best friends, but this was the first time he'd seen him in the flesh; all his dry-skinned, stretch-marked flesh. He wore a white shirt that had been crisply ironed into right angles along the seams. It made him look like a giant, bald, bespectacled box.

Not that Theo cared how he looked. It was Ian's voice he struggled with. He kept hearing him as a stranger, unable to resolve his high-pitched whine with his forty-eight-page exposé proving how the Chinese government controlled the weather.

"Fuck off," heckled a broad-shouldered man from the front of the pub. His voice slurred with anger and alcohol. He was wearing a high-vis construction vest from his day job, as if sitting on his barstool were a dangerous activity.

Theo's crowd of introverts shifted uncomfortably, a scent of shame fermenting with their default smell of damp clothes left in the washing machine for too long. Theo cleared his throat again and clenched the totem in his jacket pocket for strength.

"I am a rational man," he said.

"Could you speak up, please?" said a nasal voice from the back. The surrounding din was drowning him out.

"I am a rational man," Theo said, louder. Maybe the loudest he'd ever spoken before. "And you all too, by being here this evening, are also rational men." He was used to speaking softly, politely. But here, now, the increased volume made him feel physically larger. Each decibel was an extra pound of mass. Then he remembered that someone had brought their mum. "Rational *people*," he corrected. She was busy on her phone. "But these ... these are irrational times."

A few people in the audience nodded. Ian made a shrill murmur in agreement.

"But what does it mean, to be rational people in irrational times?" Theo continued, trying to moderate the full-bodied words flowing from him, testing the power of his voice. "I'm not sure I know myself, but I know the answer, whatever it is, will be very important. To find it is why we're all here. To save the world."

"Fucking loon," said the luminous man over his shoulder at the bar. The insult deflected off Theo's ears. He was so focused on his speech, no heckle could derail him. Audrey had been right. His tunnel vision *was* his greatest strength.

"We all have questions," Theo said, clearly, confidently. "Was Mother Teresa actually a Russian agent? Could planet Earth be trapezoid in shape? WHO really is intercepting Eric's mail?"

He had read it was always good to include a joke in your opening. Theo paused for the knowing laughter. They had recently discovered that the World Health Organization was withholding Eric's exotic magazine subscriptions.

"I haven't slept for nine days," whimpered Eric in the middle row.

"People will tell you these questions aren't important. That we should focus on what's right in front of us. Live your lives. Don't bother yourselves with what you can't change.

"*They* don't understand. Yes, these are big questions. So big they seem almost redundant to ask. But I assure you their implications filter down. And up. Sideways! Into everything. These questions *are* right in front of us. And I can't live anymore pretending they aren't."

Theo had been gesturing with a Biro. He noticed both the Jack Russell and a man in the front row had become transfixed on its point. He put the pen in his pocket. He didn't want anything to distract from his speech. He didn't want anything to hide behind. Not anymore.

"That's why I set up this in-person group. I've been writing my newsletter a long time now. Seven years. And from that has spawned this incredible Truthinati community." He identified a man in the front row by his neatly written name tag. "*TheJohnAvenger*, you and I have been investigating commercial plane routes for eighteen months. I've never encountered a more thorough, aviation-orientated mind."

TheJohnAvenger rose to his feet slowly. His dreadlocks slithered up the back of his chair like tentacles. His leather pilot's jacket was decorated with patches he'd designed himself: *Area 51 Clearance, Bilderberg Hunter Division, Powerpuff Girls Fan Club President.*

"AND I'VE NEVER MET A MORE COMPASSIONATE, CONSIDERATE SOUL," *TheJohnAvenger* said, far too loudly for the size of the audience. Decades of illegal planespotting at Heathrow Airport's second runway had ruined his hearing. "YOU *LISTEN* TO ME."

"It's hard not to when you speak, *JohnAvenger*," Theo said. The audience chuckled.

TheJohnAvenger cupped his ear. "WHAT?"

Theo searched the crowd of fourteen and found a short man with a bowl haircut. His fringe brushed the top of his white-framed spectacles. "I first met you, *QuriousGeorge*, just after the pop singer Beyoncé announced she was pregnant. In just five short months, you, I, and a few others managed to prove it was a fake, uncovering the stork farms that celebrities and politicians use to have surrogate births."

QuriousGeorge stood up. He wasn't much taller than when he was sitting down. "Now they know!" he said in a gruff voice, his bowl hair swaying from side to side.

Theo outstretched a palm to a bright ginger-haired man in the front row. They locked hands firmly, faithfully.

"*SnailsArentReal9*. The man, the myth, the legend. I might not agree with you on everything, but I treasure our debates into the night." The two men released each other's hands. "Thank you so much for coming to be here with us. Everyone, *Snails* has traveled all the way from Basingstoke this evening!"

The crowd lightly applauded. That was at least a ninety-minute drive in weekday traffic.

One of the followers leaned over to *Snails* as he sat down. "What's your username about?"

"Snails ... ," *SnailsArentReal9* said, unblinking. "They're not real."

"Really?"

"They're cameras."

"All of them?"

"Every godforsaken one."

Theo put his hands to his mouth in prayer. The tips of his index fingers rested on his lips. "I've saved the best until last." He motioned to his confidant in the second row. "Stand up, please, Ian."

Ian rose with the grace of a self-loading pallet truck. He was terrified of public speaking. His cheeks trembled in fear.

"I couldn't have done any of this without you," said Theo. "The newsletter, this first meetup, what we're going to do next … you're not just my general. You're my best friend."

Theo walked over to Ian and took him in a heavy embrace. Despite being the much larger man, Ian wilted in Theo's arms. He held him tightly, like Theo was the only lifeline away from his crushingly mediocre life.

The followers sat in silent awe.

Theo returned to the front of his audience. He looked in each of their eyes, and they met his gaze with unconscious, hopeful pride. This was the first time many of them had ever been able to hold sustained eye contact for years. Theo's strength didn't only come from inside of him; it also came from them listening to him.

His throat gently vibrated. He could feel his voice, confident and full-bodied, even before he spoke.

"We know our favorite questions: Is the moon actually a two-dimensional object? Does New Zealand actually exist? Who really is the popstar Selena Gomez, and could she be the missing four-year-old girl Samantha Hollybush, who was abducted from her home fifteen years ago?" Theo raised his arms in front of him. The totem in his jacket pocket poked him in his chest, playing his rib cage like a xylophone. "And biggest of all … how can we save the world?"

Theo lowered his arms. The followers followed the motion with their eyes. He waited until they returned to look at him.

"I'll take a pint of Bishop's and a pork pie, mate," said a man at the bar.

"But there's a bigger question we have to answer before any of that, if we ever want to make a change." His right fist clenched, grasping at the intangible waves of energy that flowed through him, as though he could hold the very vibrations in his heart.

"We've got to stop asking 'why' to each other all the time. Instead, to take our mission mainstream, we need to listen to the common man. *Nobody* listens to them anymore. These people who get up early, who work long, hard days, who come home when the sun is long gone, their houses are cold and their food has become just fuel. It drains you. There's no *why* in a life like that. You just do what you do because that's what's done. It's what your dad did. What his dad did. What your kid will do. You're trapped in a system designed by the real people in control."

Theo sensed a shift of luminous movement in his peripherals.

"We can't ask them 'why' anymore. We've got to ask ourselves 'how.' How do we make people care?"

He let his eyes float over the three rows of occupied orange plastic chairs, to the car park of the Marksman, and the world beyond.

"It's simple. We listen to them, and they'll listen to us."

THEN

Audrey hid sweltering in her car, dead in the middle of a supermarket car park. The sun stabbed at her through its engorged windscreen. It was the hottest day of the year, and the radio said it was making people crazy.

She was about to lead her first *real* scientific study. No pop psychology. No shortcuts. Just her and the thrill of discovery. And also hopefully world-changing fame and glory. It was exciting, the first tangible action from her university-scribbled manifesto. This was what she wanted to do with her life.

It was a shame, then, that she currently couldn't breathe.

A black Toyota crept across her rearview mirror. The car park was full, and it wanted her space. Her chest rose and fell rapidly, trying to force air into her lungs. She made eye contact with the driver. He had the head of a tomato, red all over with several strands of hair sprouting out the top. She could see an angry vein pulsing on his forehead. The tomato realized she wasn't moving and swore at her. Audrey used what little breath she could inhale to inflate a middle finger in his direction. The car jerked away.

The forecast had said there would be no rain for weeks. There were hosepipe bans in the Southeast. People were asked to keep showers to four minutes. The prime minister appealed to the nation on daytime TV to turn the taps off while they brushed their teeth. The country had a plan to deal with a water drought. Slightly tipsy on the rising mercury, because who needs gin when you've got 100-proof heatstroke, Audrey thought England should have countermeasures for when there's a drought of good ideas too.

She tugged upward on the window handle, trying to separate herself from the reality outside. Some nights, she would dream of electric windows, gliding up and down through the air at the touch of a button. She still had the secondhand car her grandad bought her when she first left for university. He couldn't afford the fanciest mod cons like power steering, fuel efficiency, and an engine that started the first time. He couldn't afford any car, for that matter. But she had gotten into Canterbury, and he lived in Southampton. He used his state pension to buy his granddaughter the best car he could not afford. He skipped dinner every evening that winter to pay off the credit card. Even at his age, he believed you couldn't leave life with debts still owed.

Audrey was pulled from her thoughts by movement in her rearview. The black Toyota was back. The man's eyes bulged and twitched behind its wheel. She could hear the talk radio wafting out, no doubt raising his temperature as much as the hot, humid air. She shut her eyes and asked Christ for rain to cool everyone down. If she believed in that kind of thing.

HOOOOOORN, shouted the car rudely.

Audrey heard the electric lowering of his window. "Shit or get off the pot!" he ranted.

Why am I even here? she thought, half delirious with dehydration, the other half with a building panic attack. Her body odor had turned stagnant and sat heavy in the front seat beside her. That was Stephen's seat. She preferred the BO. She thought about being refreshed. Refreshed by the rain. Refreshed by the break. Refreshed by a boyfriend who would support you when you told him you were anxious about your first big experiment, rather than saying, "You can always fall back on teaching."

She didn't want to *fall back*. She wanted to fall forward. Face-first if needs be.

Refresh-*ments*! she remembered. She was at the supermarket to get refreshments. Crisps, fizzy drinks, sweets. If Audrey had learned anything from months and months of repetitive interviews, the most important logistic for success was intermittently spaced snacks—

Her head whipped forward hard onto the dashboard. Her nose snapped. The taste of liquid iron pooled in the back of her throat. The world through the windscreen sloshed from side to side, but the dashboard remained utterly still. Looking down, she saw blood drip onto her chest. *Her* blood. The first few red dots dissipated instantly into her sweat like raindrops on a sea. Then the ocean saturated and turned crimson. Audrey slowly brought her head up, trying to still her disorientated vision. She stared at the man in the black Toyota. His fat forehead wrinkled in panic.

The bastard rammed me.

He leaned out his window. This was his chance to apologize. To say he didn't mean it. To explain it's a hot day and his son woke up sick and he's got to get more Pepto-Bismol to try to stop him constantly throwing up. He's so worried about him. It's the first time he's ever gotten *really* sick like this. He just wanted to stop his vomiting, if only for a few hours, so his son could get some sleep.

Or he could double down.

"It's a car park, you bitch! Not a coffee shop. People need spaces! That's the problem with this country! People are taking up English people's spaces!"

Audrey's eyes filled with tears. These were not tears of emotion, though. It was important for her to note that. This man had not affected her. Confusing parking etiquette with immigration policy had not affected her. Stephen had not affected her. This was simply an autonomous response to her nose breaking.

Her breathing started to come easier. She was thinking clearly again. All it took was a minor car crash. Several ideas in her head had been bumped into one coherent thought: *physical triggers cause seemingly emotional reactions.*

Her silence made the tomato even angrier, hotter. She wiped her nose with the back of her hand. Blood smeared across the top of her lip and flicked down her cheek. The man reached inside his car and honked the HOOOORN every few words like he had a real-time censorship device.

"Do you *HOOORN* know how many *HOOORN* cars there are backed up the A12 because *HOOORN* like you aren't moving on *HOOORN* quick enough?"

She watched him in the mirror. His eyes were bulging. He was doing little hops up and down as he sounded the horn. His free arm swung wildly, occasionally punching the wing mirror. He looked like he had all the power because he was shouting the loudest. But if a man yells in a car park and everyone ignores him, does he actually make a sound?

Audrey pulled the rearview mirror down so she could only see her own reflection. She was grinning widely, blood lining the spaces between her teeth, blood covering the bottom half of her face, red dots on her shirt.

He could go fuck himself, for all she cared. She had the power. She wasn't listening.

NOW

Phil's high-vis jacket glinted through the torrential rain from across the road. In the months since what his followers were now calling the Sermon for the Marks, Theo had never seen him take it off. Phil stood opposite the pub, hair plastered to his forehead, watching their livestream test on his phone.

He shot a muscled arm up into the sky. His thumb flicked up like a switchblade.

"Looks and sounds great, boss," he shouted through the storm.

Theo nodded and went inside, downstairs, into the cellar of the Marksman. Amongst the casks of real ale was a makeshift studio. The landlord, Colin, believed so much in Theo's message that he had converted the basement for free. The set's desk was made from the pub toilet's broken door resting on two kegs of lager for legs. A foldout chair from the garden sat behind it. Phil had made a green screen by dyeing his mother's bedspread with luminous paint he bought online. He had convinced Ian to overlay a World War II bunker background for the broadcast. And Theo, having never had a paying job, asked his father for £150 to buy a camera. He gave Theo £300 to leave him alone. Theo obliged, thankful for his father's support.

Destiny provided the rest.

They had found an old condenser microphone on the floor in the corner of the basement, the kind Elvis hollered into before he was abducted by aliens. A metallic oblong box the size of a fist, its sound packed just as much of a punch. Horizontal slits cut across its body like intergalactic android visors. It was always cold to the touch. Colin said he'd never seen it before, and he took over the place in 2004. The microphone took on a mythologically powerful status amongst the group, as it was a likely example of quantum wall diffusion theory.

The quantum wall (confusingly named after the groundbreaking television drama *The Qunt Dynasty*, rather than any actual link to quantum physics) was the barrier between realities. Theo had long feared this interdimensional defense had weakened, exposing their Earth to attack. The microphone was the latest piece of proof—like the sudden reappearance of the Eiffel Tower in 1954 (despite being used as Hitler's Nazi escape rocket to Neptune a decade prior) and Phil's dad leaving for the shops when Phil was four years old, to never be seen again.

Unfortunately, the quantum wall now had more gaps than the so-called "ozone layer." *Snails* said it was more leaky than the Swedish Embassy, which had made them laugh so much, the group used that comparison whenever they could. Your roof in the rain is more leaky than the Swedish Embassy, Colin. Your mum's Sunday roast has more leeks than the Swedish Embassy, Phil. You really should consult a doctor, Ian, because you're taking more leaks than the Swedish Embassy.

But these were the halcyon days of a world-changing movement, when a subliminal cultural invasion from the Swedish Embassy was the worst of their problems.

Tucked away in the shadows behind the camera, cramped in with half-used paint tins, a trolley, and several boxes of Colin's old *Amateur Photographer* magazines from the mid-90s, sat Ian and a laptop extending with wires.

"Vic-*tor*. Whis-*key*," said Ian, holding the microphone delicately, nearing his full recital of the phonetic alphabet. He pronounced each syllable in whiney clips.

"Coming right up." Theo smiled, passing him a tumbler overflowing with whiskey and Coke. He had a mug of tea for himself, which he always took black. He tried to avoid the dairy industry these days, who were enriching cow milk with salamander estrogen to control the national birth rate. "Phil says it's all coming through clear."

Ian took a long sip. His hand was trembling.

"It needs to be perfectly clear," he said.

"It is."

"There can't be any lags or dropped frames or—"

"There won't be."

"Because if Phil is just saying it's okay to stitch us up for when we do go live—"

"He isn't."

The accountant put his hands over his face and inhaled four asthmatic breaths. He threw his hands down and looked up at Theo with reddened, pleading eyes. "What if no one listens to us?"

Theo put a hand on his shoulder. "If we listen to them, they'll listen to us."

Ian looked past Theo at Phil dripping down the cellar steps. "That's what I'm worried about," he said under his wheezing breath.

Theo took the microphone over to the desk and sat down. He swiveled the mic into its stand, testing its range of motion, a runner warming up before the marathon ahead, because he knew just like that first race in ancient Greece to save Atlantis, he needed to deliver a message to save a civilization. He stroked his hand across the tabletop. Smooth, empty: a blank slate. He reached his hand down into the bag under his chair, hidden from Ian, Phil, and the webcam's red dot eye, and touched the object inside. His forefinger rested in the totem's hollow groove.

He felt the confidence spread through his body. His voice box vibrated.

They had decided to call the channel *HearRational*.

He sat forward.

"Let's go live."

THEN

A man—*why is it always a man?* she wrote in her notepad—sat across from Audrey in a silly hat.

The silly hat was her idea. It was a device for Audrey to read minds. Not in the way her subjects thought reading minds worked. She couldn't tell what they were thinking about, or subliminally command them to assassinate the home secretary. But the hat did show her patterns in brain waves, how intensely they occurred, and in which part of the brain.

It was covered in diodes and electrodes and wires. A cold metal rim wrapped around the man's cranium, two brown fluffy pads placed on his temples. Three copper beams went up and over the top of his head, with more pads attaching to his scalp. All subjects were required to shave their heads for the experiment to get the most accurate readings. None of them had objected. Their hair was mostly gone anyway.

Inverse correlation between hair follicles and conspiracy theories? she scribbled down. She suppressed a snigger.

The device's cooling box whirred like an asthma attack as she switched it on. The red and blue diodes blinked as they awoke; the bitter smell of overdone toast wafted from the motor box. Audrey checked the pads were correctly positioned. As she looked down at her subject's head, she thought of it as a theater of the faulty mind; the hat's metal beams were the stadium's structural supports, the mechanical hum its capacity crowd of excited psychology fans.

Go, Doc-tor Lowe! Go! Go!

Audrey only knew the man as Subject 64. Anonymity was vital. She, or the integrity of the experiment, couldn't be contaminated by their identities. Particularly a subject like Subject 64, who droned on in the high-pitched whine of faraway traffic.

"Nobody talks about the water erosion of the Eiffel Tower! These—these Eiffel Tower experts, they all say that the Eiffel Tower has been there for over 130 years. All that time, and that it's never moved. *Never.* That's—that's impossible. Do you know why?"

Audrey made sure neither to nod nor shake her head. It was also vital not to indulge in any of the subjects' fantasies. She simply repeated back what Subject 64 had already told her.

"The water erosion?"

"The water erosion on the Eiffel Tower! The Eiffel Tower experts, they've—they've—they've constructed whole careers out of matchsticks. Not the wrought-iron latticework of the structure they study. They believe that the Eiffel Tower has been in Paris for the 134 years since it was built. But they believe their own beliefs too much. They're trapped, trapped in their own Eiffel Tower theories where they write books on the Eiffel and do Eiffel lecture tours and host Eiffel podcasts, getting trapped in a 330-meter-high lie they can't even see anymore, because they've spent the last twenty, thirty years of their lives only looking up, never down. If they even consider the water erosion of the Eiffel Tower, it's not just their ideas that are for nothing; it's their whole *careers.*"

Audrey had been listening to Subject 64 drone on about water erosion for three consecutive sessions. If nonsense was water, she knew how the Eiffel Tower felt.

"There is no evidence of water erosion on the Eiffel Tower in the nine years between 1945 and 1954. Do you think the peacetime following World War II brought about a decade of summer? No! Hitler used it as an escape rocket."

Audrey strained her eyes to stop them from rolling.

"The textbooks are *lying* about the Eiffel Tower, and everyone just gets on with their lives like lying about the Eiffel Tower isn't a big deal, like nothing else could be a lie too. Because what they don't say about the Eiffel Tower, what they ignore, *willfully* ignore, is the water erosion of the Eiffel Tower. The grooves from the water erosion on the Eiffel Tower prove it went missing for nine years, because of the rain. They've had a geologist confirm it. You can see it, can't you, that you can't ignore when truth leaves a mark? A physical, tangible mark!"

Audrey's eyes drifted past Subject 64. She thought of the man in the car park the previous month, and how she shut him out. She absentmindedly touched her nose where it had snapped and watched a boring blue sky that still hadn't broken shimmer in the heat. Not a single cloud floated beyond the window. She longed for a spot of bad weather.

She refocused. She fixed her eyes on Subject 64 and zoomed in on the bead of sweat running from his brow. *The water erosion of the Eiffel Tower.* This was the start of her life's work. She wouldn't get a second chance. Everything needed to be rigorous, honed, concentrated. *Imagine the satisfaction, Audrey, of an experiment done right.* Of a hypothesis proved. Of Dr. Worthington suggesting she pitch her study to the pop press with the title *"Non, Je Ne Regrette Rien* of a Paranoid Schizophrenic," and her politely explaining that she didn't do hack headlines anymore. Of not being dragged down by the gravitational pull of Stephen's mediocrity.

But, also, she had never heard someone say the words *Eiffel Tower* so many times in one continuous breath. It had started to sound like *trifle*, in more ways than one. Each repetition was another Chinese water torture drop.

Her eyes flicked between Subject 64 and the chunky computer. Subject 64 didn't know this, but his real-time brain scans when he spoke about the alleged disappearance of the Eiffel Tower were the exact same patterns from their first session, when he recalled walking in on his mother having an affair with the local butcher as a child, and how he felt threatened by his erect penis.

She stifled a laugh.

"It's the water erosion of the Eiffel Tower," Subject 64 whimpered, breaking Audrey's mind from its distraction. His eyes had become reddened, pleading. "Life leaves a mark on everything."

*On every*one, Audrey thought.

NOW

The camera's red light blinked, blinked, blinked, stayed on. Its eye was open and already sore.

Ian made a disproportionately small thumbs-up, his face fading behind the red livestream light.

Theo cleared his throat and remembered his first audience in the pub. He had no plan for what he said back then. He'd learned over the last six months that sometimes what you said wasn't actually the important part. Making people listen was what mattered.

He pulled the interdimensional microphone toward his lips.

"I am Theo Papadopoulos," he said into the damp quiet of the Marksman cellar. His concentration focused. He was now utterly alone and talking to everyone.

"Welcome to my channel, *HearRational*," he said, remembering the manners his grandmother had taught him. He gestured to a chair out of shot, as though his digital guest could sit down. "Please come in and make yourself at home."

Ian had made him practice his speech over and over the day before they went live. But even though nothing had changed besides the red light now being on, Theo felt a notable difference. It was no longer just his voice box that felt charged; it was the very basement air he breathed. It was as though his message, his *voice*, had finally found the megaphone it needed.

"Now would be the part of the video where I'd ask you to subscribe. To leave a comment and enable notifications. I'm not going to ask you to do that. In fact, I don't *want* you to do that. I want you to start thinking consciously, actively, about the decisions you make. I want you to start taking control of your own lives."

Theo wheeled back his chair slightly and pointed to the luminous green bedspread draped behind him. The viewers would see stock video of the globe slowly rotating, its surface covered in microchip city lights.

"The first, and only, place you can really take control is how you perceive the world. Our minds have become cluttered and full up. We've been given everything, way more than we need, and it has cluttered the rooms in our head. Yes, the mind is a big place with lots of storage. But it's nothing when faced with a whole world of ideas and beliefs. Our heads are a mess, and a clean slate is long overdue.

"But how do you empty your mind of all its cultural and ideological waste? Easy." Theo smiled warmly. "All you need to do is to question everything."

Ian clicked his mouse. The globe backdrop cut to a picture of a giant red question mark.

"First question: What should my first question be?

"That's what I'm here for, fellow traveler. Your first question should be: Who are you to be telling me what to think?" Theo chuckled. He now always made sure to include a disarming joke before his more challenging ideas.

"I am a rational man in irrational times. I'm a man who's been told wrong answers to the right questions all my life. I'm a man who's tugged at the loose threads of reality and has seen it unravel. Simply put, the answer is: I am you.

"I'll ask you a question now, in return. Are you satisfied with the way our world works? Are you and your kin content with corrupt politicians and greedy CEOs and hypocritical scientists and lying journalists and vacuous celebrities and never-right economists and patronizing teachers? Do you mind that the very planet we live on feels like it's trying to get rid of us?

"My apologies, that was more than one question. That's the thing with the good ones, though. They don't much give answers. They give more questions.

"You'll find that out soon enough."

Ian clicked again. The video backdrop returned to the rotating globe. Only this time it was red, and its pretty city lights replaced by fire.

"There's a war coming, whoever is listening. But it's not for land or power or silicon chips. It's for the truth. It's for who gets to decide what truth is. And I don't know about you, but I promised myself a long time ago the only person who decides my truth ... is me."

Theo nodded to the bottom corner of his frame, inviting Earth to join him.

"Now is when I ask you all, if you want to save the world, subscribe."

CHAPTER 2:
TAKE A CHANCE, TAKE A CHANCE, TAKE A CHA-CHA-CHANCE ON ME: HOW REPETITION AND CHARISMA MANIPULATE THE MEDIA

The pads were sodden sponges, heavy with Subject 64's sweat. Audrey threw the single-use pads in the bin and washed her hands in the bathroom. Her skin had dried and cracked from doing this same process over and over and over.

Reentering the main room, she jumped. A teenage boy sat in Subject 64's place, the headset already on top of his shaved head. He must've actually had hair to shave.

"You must be—" She hurried over to her notes to check his name, forgetting that's not how this experiment worked. The people she listened to had no name. The boy, to her, was just *Subject 88*. Fifteen years old, baby-faced, parental consent form signed. She shuffled some papers to appear busy. They didn't need shuffling.

"Good morning," the boy said politely, offering his hand. She shook it. It wasn't greasy. He was the youngest participant she'd interviewed so far. She checked the parental consent form again. Signed. The emerging sandpaper bristles on his head made him look like a monk. "May I ask your name? Mine's—"

Audrey threw her hands over her ears to block his voice. "No! Don't tell me your name! I can't know it."

She saw Subject 88's lips mouth *I'm sorry*.

Audrey lowered her hands. "No, I'm sorry. You don't have to apologize." Months of interviewing socially inept conspiracy theorists had rubbed off on her. She relaxed her shoulders. She hadn't realized how bunched they'd become. "You're a very polite young man," she said, and then cringed at sounding like a very polite old woman.

"Thank you," said Subject 88, sitting back down. He searched her face. "Are you okay?"

Audrey was taken aback. The eighty-seven other subjects had asked her many questions. Who was *really* behind this experiment? Was she aware of the water erosion of the Eiffel Tower? Some utter nonsense about snails. Three months ... and not a single one had asked her a question about herself. Granted, that's not the point of a controlled experiment. But lead scientists are people too.

She didn't reply. What would she have answered? *Yes? No? Depends on how drunk I got last night to ignore my fiancé?*

"I only ask because your nose ... it's bleeding."

Audrey grabbed a tissue and dabbed at her nostrils. Her nose liked to occasionally gush blood every now and then since the car park crash. Stephen said you can't call a several-mile-per-hour bump a "crash." *Life leaves a mark*, echoed Subject 64's voice, as though he were a mystic ghost guiding her with social media style affirmations.

Audrey scrunched the crimson tissue into the ball of her hand. "I'm very sorry about that."

Subject 88 chuckled. "No need. My little brother gets nose-bleeds all the time. I can sometimes find him by following the red dots on the carpet."

"I'm like that, but with wine," Audrey joked unintentionally. She was supposed to have staged, sterilized, standardized conversations, not actual ones. She tried to smother the situation in small talk. "Your brother must be very bad at hide-and-seek."

"Yes, very. He's dead."

Audrey dropped the tissue on the floor. It unfurled like a blooming rose. "Oh, I'm so sorry. I just, I thought because you spoke in present tense ..."

"That's my mistake," said Subject 88. "It's confusing for people sometimes. He is considered"—he made air quotes—"'dead' in our dimension, but his consciousness is being held captive in an alternate reality."

"Right," said Audrey, remembering she had specifically designed the online recruitment ads to target people with "fringe beliefs" and "suggestions of brain trauma." She was surprised those were already default criteria you could tick.

Subject 88's eyes suddenly became large, lost, innocent. "The advert said you would be able to help me save him."

It did not. The advert was in no way that specific. *Sign up NOW to save your dead brother trapped in an alternate dimension!* Audrey wasn't going to correct him, though. She liked the sound of her helping people.

"This experiment is to help you and people like you," she said. "To help the world understand what you believe to be true." Not a lie, just *open for interpretation.*

Subject 88's eyes squinted like he was trying to read a faraway sign.

"I want to help other people," he said.

That was an odd reply, Audrey thought. But he had just mentioned interdimensional soul kidnapping, so relatively, it was fine.

"Let me just check that headset is on correctly." She walked around him to inspect the pad positioning. She noticed a faint scar almost hidden by the wires on the back of his skull. "Very good job ... I'm just going to ask you some test questions to get a baseline reading for the software."

Subject 88 nodded.

"What day is it today?"

"Tuesday. Two fifteen p.m."

"Great. The sky is blue, true or false?"

"False," Subject 88 said.

Audrey looked up. In three months, nobody had said false.

Subject 88 motioned to the window. "It's gray."

Audrey turned. She would call it "bluey gray." Because, finally, after sixteen long weeks, the sky had broken. The first drops of rain gently splashed against the window.

"So it is," she said.

She sat back and considered the boy more carefully. He was tall for his age. Pale, yes, but not in an unhealthy way. In a purer sense. *Like a wedding dress*, was the only comparison her mind served up.

Audrey checked the reading. The machine said he was telling the truth. Or, at least, he believed he was.

"What's your favorite subject at school?"

"Science."

"And why's that?"

"I like all the questions."

"Not the answers?" Audrey smiled.

Subject 88 grimaced, shuffled in his seat, as though the concept of answers was too loud for his ears. "They're okay, I guess. For some people." His eyes found her. "Are they enough for you?"

Audrey absentmindedly tapped a pen on her temple. The scientific process was all about controlling variables. Limit as many differences in the experiment as possible. But she had been asking the same questions eight times a day for three monotonous months. *She* wanted to be listened to for a change.

Audrey put her pen down. "Answers are overrated."

Subject 88's face softened into curiosity. "Then what are you trying to do here?"

"I'm trying to prove someone else's answers wrong."

"Whose?"

Audrey sat back. "Where to start? The scientific community, my PhD advisor, or my fiancé?"

Audrey's joke left a chemtrail over his head.

"The scientific community's, please."

"Well, there's this prevailing belief in my field of psychology that people who have their own ... extraordinary beliefs, people like you, believe those things not because the theories have merit, but because they have a personality that falls into the set of traits we call schizotypy."

"Schi-zo-ty-py," Subject 88 recited, logging the word in his mind.

Audrey did a thumbs-up. "Nailed the pronunciation. It's a personality type that ranges from magical thinking to, well, to psychosis."

"That's why I really wanted to be involved in your study," said Subject 88, sitting forward. "You're trying to prove what I've experienced is real, so we can warn the world about the invasion. I respect that."

Audrey bit her lip.

Subject 88 continued: "I think it would be useful to know what the traits of—" He slowed down. "—*Schi-zo-ty-py* are."

"Of course." Audrey opened the *Diagnostic and Statistical Manual of Mental Disorders (Fifth Edition)* beside her, scanned through to find the word of the day. "The personality traits are:

Paranoid or suspicious thinking

Eccentricity

Low trust in others

A strong need to feel special

Belief that the world is a dangerous place

And seeing meaningful patterns where none exist."

Audrey looked up at Subject 88 from over her book. "Do you have any of these traits?"

"I do see meaningful patterns. How about you?"

Audrey read the definition again in her head. *Full marks.* Maybe she should do the experiment on herself. She shut the book.

"My apologies, I've gone off on a bit of a tangent. Let's return to the prepared questions. Please tell me about a strong belief you hold that others close to you disagree with."

NOW

"A species of interdimensional vampires has infiltrated our governments, and they are stealing your deceased loved ones' souls for their bloodsucking energy."

Theo was pleased with how quickly his audience was accepting his more challenging theories. He had expected a similar rate of progress as his newsletter, which had taken over half a decade to build up. He was prepared for a multi-year mission. Yet in just three months of daily broadcasts, he had passed fifty thousand subscribers with a regular live audience of 1,800. Real-time video, he realized, was far better at getting people to listen than the written word.

A limb shook in the dark behind the makeshift studio lights. It was Ian gesturing at the tablet on the desk. A Vietnamese tech company had sent it to Theo as a gift with a letter explaining how excited they were for his travel/gaming/beauty/lifestyle vlog. They called him a microinfluencer.

Theo glanced at its screen. There was a username, followed by the number fifty. "Thank you, *HopeForever0*. That's a very generous donation. Your question is: *Do you fear the power of God?*"

Theo sat back. In the years and years he had been developing his theories, he had never addressed the idea of religion or a God. To him, the notion of an all-powerful, omnipotent being that had created existence was an ecclesial step too far. He had more realistic, science-based beliefs, like how the world was controlled by *The Ten Men*, a secret committee made up of two heads of state, seven CEOs of multinational conglomerates, and the rapper-turned-business mogul Jay-Z. With logic like that, Theo didn't need faith.

Perhaps Theo had blocked God because of those long Orthodox sermons he and Benny had to sit through as children, perched on uncomfortable wooden pews with flat cushions for your knees while you prayed. Benny once asked their father why God made the seats at church so uncomfortable. Their father explained that God created cushions a little after he did churches, and everyone had decided to keep things traditional. Benny was good at asking questions that showed how people didn't really know why they did the things they did. Theo missed him greatly.

He could feel his brain contract and expand like a muscle over *HopeForever0*'s question, working at solving a puzzle just beyond his comprehension. Now that he pondered it, God, the Devil, Heaven, Hell, perhaps that was just another version of the same world-threatening plot.

"Do I fear the power of God?" he intoned again. "I fear any power. Anyone who says otherwise doesn't understand the nature of power. But that doesn't mean I back down from it. There is no bravery in standing up to a force you do not fear.

"But maybe you mean in the sense of 'do I believe in God?' I'll be truthful, I've never given it much thought, strange as that may sound. God, or whatever name you give to that entity, I suppose the true answer is: I do not know, and nobody can.

"There will be people who tell you there is no God because there's no evidence for Him or Her or Them in the observable world.

"I imagine, then, that you point to everything around you. The air that we breathe, the fish in the sea, the stars sleeping in the sky. *Is that not enough?* you might ask your doubter.

"Ironically, they will cling to their stance, despite having the same lack of evidence as you. But do not judge them. That's the point of belief. It is an idea with parts missing."

"Ghosts are real," said Subject 88. The headset fan had slowed to a background whir.

Audrey checked the readings. He believed what he said.

"What first made you hold this belief?"

"I spoke to one."

Audrey nodded. "Please tell me what happened."

"I heard my younger brother's voice from his box."

"And your brother had passed?"

"Yes."

"What do you mean by 'his' box?"

"It's an ossuary. My family is Orthodox Christian. After a few years, they take the bones out of the ground and put them in a box."

"And that is kept in your house?"

"We're not meant to. But yes."

Audrey made a note. *Family history of disobedience.* "Please continue."

"I heard his voice, but from a distance, muffled through many walls. Far more walls than there were in the house. It was last February, and I was alone, and it was already dark by late afternoon. I walked upstairs, trying to hear the voice get louder. I was very scared. When I opened my father's wardrobe, I could hear Benny's voice much clearer. It was coming from his box."

"May I ask how your brother died?"

"Of course. My father killed him."

Audrey gasped.

"Not intentionally. It was two winters back, the one where it was so cold, going outside made your eyeballs feel full of needles. It never snowed, but the roads were always covered in ice. Most of the patches you could see, but the dangerous ones were invisible."

"Black ice," said Audrey, and felt a shiver in her bones.

"My father was driving Benny to his swimming lessons. I was top set by then, while Benny was still in the Snappers class, so we went on different days. My dad was always so careful with everything. He had the winter tires on, the car got serviced at the start of every season, he cleaned and checked it every Sunday after church. But some things you can't prepare for."

"Your father survived?"

"He didn't die."

"And you?"

"I was at home." Theo rubbed the faint line where his forehead met his shaved hair. "I had a migraine, so I didn't go swimming that week."

Audrey was almost overcome by an urge to stroke Subject 88's head for him. She suppressed it.

"You were telling me about your brother's box."

Theo closed his eyes to find where he left off. "I never liked the box," he said, opening them again. "I didn't much like the idea of him being cold and under six feet of dirt either, though. At least in the box he would be with us. Gone, but with us. But that didn't mean I liked the box. It creeped me out. I avoided it all the time. I think my dad did too, which was why it was at the bottom of his wardrobe under a load of old coats that smelt of dust. If he really wanted to avoid it, I always thought he should have put it in the attic. He would've had to open that wardrobe, knowing Benny was there, every day. But he never moved it. I guess it was like a lot of things in our house since Benny died. He was right there, and nobody talked about it. Because nobody could bring themselves to listen."

Theo closed his eyes.

"Before I go to bed, I like to replay the last time I saw him alive, before he got in the car with my dad, like tomorrow morning when I wake up, they'll pull into the driveway. Then I could just be ignorant of the impending end of the world." Theo's lids lifted halfway and found Audrey's eyes. She suddenly felt as though they were peering at each other through the slats of a confession box. She couldn't say for sure which side she was on. "I find it difficult to take that on sometimes."

"I can imagine."

Theo rubbed his eyes and sat back.

"That February, when I heard Benny's voice, that was the first time I'd looked at the ossuary since we'd snuck it home after the funeral. It had only been a few weeks since I'd last seen it, but it had taken on a totally different appearance in my mind. It was much bigger, and a different color, and there were little ornate carvings of a forest on the lid. But when I lifted off my father's winter jacket, I saw it was actually small. It was the size of a shoebox. It had a little gold metal latch and a still-fresh engraving that said *Benny*. But otherwise, it was just a normal wooden box ..."

Subject 88 trailed off, his eyes drifting through the window at a sky that wasn't blue.

"And the voice ..." Audrey anxiously checked the red recording light. "What was it saying?"

"Help," Subject 88 answered, matter-of-factly. "They're draining me."

A red dot took aim between Theo's eyes. The cameraman told him to smile so he could focus on his teeth. Theo was smiling already, as he was very keen to work with the documentary crew. He beamed an even toothier grin to be as helpful as he could.

The producer, Angus Snyde, seemed as though he had never smiled in his life. His skin was gray, and it flaked around the sides of his nose. His eyes were small and beady and fierce, like the red lights above the camera lens. Theo wondered what had happened to Angus in his life to make him so angry all the time.

Angus had gotten in touch after one of Theo's livestreams, asking to make a documentary of his life. He spoke very excitedly about wanting to tell Theo's story. When Angus spoke excitedly, it meant he shouted more.

"We have no agenda," Angus yelled in the basement studio, his authority somewhat diminished by being bent double beneath the low-hanging ceiling beams. They were still in the beer cellar of the Marksman. "We are objective video journalists."

Theo had asked Barry the Boom Mic Guy why Angus was the way he was. Barry the Boom Mic Guy said it was because

Angus was working class and had a chip on his shoulder, that he worked really hard to get into Cambridge, which he tried to let you know about all the time but secretly hated he went there. Barry went to Oxford Brookes and was middle class.

"My chum got me onto your livestreams, by the way," said Barry the Boom Mic Guy. He pressed his headphones tight around his ears and swiveled the boom mic from side to side to make sure no one else was listening. He took off the cans and whispered to Theo.

"I think Angus is going to make you look like a fool. Be careful not to fall for any of his traps."

Theo nodded and gently pulled Barry the Boom Mic Guy's boom mic toward him. "It's always so nice to meet a fan," he whispered into it.

Angus continued to yell helpful quotations to his crew. "As Godard said, 'the camera is truth twenty-four frames a second.'"

"It's twenty-five frames a second in the UK," Theo corrected, concerned they would export the wrong file format and waste all their hard work. "Twenty-nine point nine seven if it's in the US."

Angus's red eyes darted at Theo. In the basement dark between lighting tests, he had the bloodsore pupils of a rat.

Barry tried to defuse the situation. "Er, yes. It's thirty frames in the US, but—"

"Twenty-nine point nine seven," Theo corrected again. He would be very upset with himself if they couldn't finish their production because of something as small as being point zero three frames out. That would really compound over the hour broadcast slot.

"Twenty-nine point nine fucking seven then," said Angus, taking a step toward Theo on every number. They ended up nose-to-nose. Theo could smell a stale service station vanilla latte on his breath.

A large orb that hung down half the height of the room switched on and bathed the basement in light. Angus's red eyes turned their normal black. He rubbed a few flakes of dry skin off the corner of his nose.

"We're making this for an online portal," he said more calmly. "It gets converted automatically. Anyway, that's beside the point. You're talking literal frames. I'm talking wisdom. Godard says the camera captures an objective truth, so we will capture you. Honestly."

"You'll capture me?"

"In recorded footage, yes."

Theo sat down at his makeshift desk and rested his right hand on the dimensionally charged condenser mic.

"I've found livestreams to be the closest to objective truth," Theo said, making small talk as they worked out the best way to unnaturally light him. "One shot, no cutting. Just the message in the real time …"

He trailed off as his eye focused on the red dot above the camera. He was generally distrustful of authority, be it people, companies, or widely agreed upon theories of reality, but he always made sure to give individuals a chance. People as a group tended toward short-term thinking. A person could go either way.

Theo thought of Audrey, the first person to ever truly listen to him. He owed her everything for her belief. He hoped Angus would be one of the good ones.

"So, what would you like me to talk about?" Theo asked. "I cover just about everything on my livestreams."

"They're very popular," Angus said, scrolling through his tablet to remind himself of the viewing figures.

"Thank you."

"But that's you through *your* lens. For the real truth, you want to be seen through another's eye. Like how the French New Wave directors took on American tropes. The outside eye can reveal more. They see what you can't."

"You think it'll help me reach more people?"

Angus's lips peeled back from his teeth as he smiled. A glint of red returned to his eyes. "Oh yes. We can certainly help with that."

"That's wonderful, thank you so much." Theo paused. "Just one more thing."

"Anything."

"Have you subscribed?"

"Yes. We had to for research purposes."

Theo made a thumbs-up gesture by his side just for himself. He was finally taking his and Audrey's findings mainstream.

Angus pushed the cameraperson out of his way, pressed the red dot himself, and started shooting.

THEN

Ever since Audrey could remember, she could spot a liar. She'd feel a lurch in her gut at Father Christmas, the owner of the haunted mansion in *Scooby-Doo*, that one family member doing interviews on the news after their daughter had gone missing. She saw them all for what they were.

The tragedy was that it never did her any good. After all, she was engaged to Stephen Pratt.

Yet even though she knew Subject 88's wild conspiracy theories were utter fiction, she found herself believing them because *he* believed himself. She found a certain escape, a sweet numbness, in letting the boy's confident nonsense wash over her.

The machine readings backed him up. He showed no physiological evidence of lying. How could she spot a liar if the liar thought they were telling the truth? Perhaps there was an argument, in psychology, for truth to be a relative term.

"Did you believe in ghosts before this?"

"No."

"Do you hold any other uncommon beliefs?"

"Nothing mythical, like unicorns or healing crystals. Just more science-based ones like quantum wall diffusion theory and how New Zealand isn't real."

Audrey bit her tongue. She had gone backpacking in New Zealand over her second-year summer at university. She and Stephen had fallen in love with its rolling Hobbity hills. They promised each other they'd emigrate there when they were old, which neither of them had brought up for years.

"Why do you believe those to be more scientific?" she asked.

Subject 88 furrowed his brow. There was an unspoken hierarchy in his online community. Aliens were far more probable than fantasy-based mythical creatures. Lightsabers were possible, magic wands were not. Having this challenged momentarily caused him to error.

"Yes, because they are more scientific," he agreed.

His reply didn't make sense, as though he had responded to something else. Audrey pressed.

"I wasn't agreeing with you. I asked *why* do you believe interdimensional vampires and New Zealand not being real are more based in science?"

She shouldn't have said she wasn't agreeing with him, she inwardly cursed. *Stay. Impartial.*

Subject 88 leaned his head slightly forward, his brow wrinkled. He was trying to hear her, but appeared as though her voice wasn't quite getting through.

He answered: "What people believe to be New Zealand was actually a movie set created for Peter Jackson's *Lord of the Rings* trilogy. If you look into it, there's no record of New Zealand anywhere until 2002."

Stephen had an aunt who had emigrated to New Zealand in 1989, but there was something intoxicating about the idea a whole country never existing, about Theo's confident delivery, about his empathetic eyes. The cognitive dissonance made her feel lightheaded. She indulged in the fantasy.

"What reason would the whole world have to pretend an antipodean country exists on the other side of the planet?"

"You can trace everything back to Them," Subject 88 said, not having yet revealed who They were. "The *Lord of the Rings* franchise is a cover story for New Zealand, which is a cover-up for a top secret military base hidden far away from everyone."

"How would you explain Australia?"

"You're right, Australia is heavily dependent on the military industrial trade that comes from Base X. Base X isn't its official name. That's just what we've called it for investigation purposes. Australia is in on it."

Audrey pulled out a crumpled newspaper from her bag. She pointed at a photograph in the world news section. "This is the prime minister of New Zealand at the United Nations this week."

Subject 88 shook his head regretfully. "She's an actor. A good one too. The lengths these organizations go to to keep their secrets."

Audrey blinked. Every rabbit hole was supported by an underground network of darker tunnels. She was so deep, she couldn't see which one they'd entered through anymore. She drew a *Q* on her notes, a reminder to explore further later on.

"When your brother first spoke to you, you said he asked for your help?"

"He told me he was trapped, and They were draining him."

"When you say They or Them, who do you mean?"

Subject 88's eyes darted to the window, spooked by the sudden flight of a sparrow.

"I don't know if I can say."

Audrey thought of all the ludicrous conspiracy theory shadow organizations she'd heard of through the years. "Is it a secret ring of child predators? The government? Lizard people?"

Subject 88 sighed. "Like all those aren't the same."

Audrey wanted to satisfy her own curiosity, to see how deep this grand unifying theory of worlds went. But she also wanted to sincerely help Subject 88. To help him distinguish reality from escapism.

She waited until Subject 88 made eye contact again. She held his gaze and asked, "Who was draining him?"

"That's not the question you should be asking."

"What is?"

Subject 88 inhaled deeply. "How can we stop Them coming for us next?"

Colin whistled as he poured a pint upstairs.

"One million subscribers," he said wistfully.

The last drinker had stumbled out of the Marksman; the doors were locked; the street was dark. Ian took a sip of his whiskey and Coke. Phil chugged half a bitter. Colin placed an ale in front of Theo. The glass knocked deeply on the wooden bar.

"Builders Lane only holds two thousand," Colin said, picturing the local football ground. "You'd need ... I don't know, you'd probably need at least twenty Lanes to hold that many subscribers."

"Just a tea, thanks, Colin," said Theo.

"Sorry, boss! I'll never get used to people in here not drinking." Colin lifted the pint back onto his side of the bar and lined it up next to his own. "This one's mine then!"

"And it would be five hundred, Colin." Theo smiled.

Colin whistled again, along with the kettle, as he made Theo an English Breakfast tea. Colin was always in awe at something. In a way, he was the perfect man behind a bar, a sympathetic ear to whatever problems or conspiracy theories his punters had. It was with that willingness to entertain all possibilities, a complete lack of uncritical thinking, that drew him into Theo's close circle. And that he ran a pub where they could have a studio rent-free.

Colin clinked the glasses of Ian and Phil and passed Theo a ceramic mug of tea. "To five hundred Builders Lanes then," he said. "And finally giving these bastards what for!"

Phil punched his fist, knuckles down, onto the bar. The glasses in the dishwasher tray rattled beneath. Theo was incredibly thankful to have found three of the best, most rational men in such dangerous, irrational times. They were all on exactly the same page: to expose the interdimensional vampire invasion before it ended the world.

Phil picked at his reddened knuckles. "We'll give those Biased Bastard Cucks what for as well," he said. "And the liberal elites. And the paedos and immigrants."

Theo nodded along with the others. It was great to know how focused everyone was on the singular interdimensional vampire threat.

"They tried to stitch you up with that program, boss," said Phil. He nodded up to the rifle on the wall behind the bar. "Let me have that gun, Colin. I'll show them how to shoot a documentary."

Colin shrugged. "It's only a replica."

"Ain't it all." Phil bitterly drank the rest of his bitter. "Just fakes everywhere. Not us, though. Not with you, Theo." He squeezed Theo's shoulder. "Anyway, the joke's on them. Their show only got us more eyeballs. Our views are through the bloody roof. It's like you say: if we listen to them, they'll listen to us."

Theo cheersed Phil's outstretched glass.

"Incredible," said Ian, hunched over a tablet. He was never without one these days, obsessively poring over analytics and insights as to how best to optimize Theo's livestream reach.

"What's that, mate?" said Phil. Ian had complained to Theo that Phil always said the word *mate* like he was saying the word *dickhead*. Theo explained he just had resting angry voice.

"In each video's analytics, you can see what sort of people are watching. What age they are, what gender they are. Where they're watching from …"

"Where we biggest, mate? I bet it's everywhere but London. That place is nothing but lefties and foreigners. And paedos."

"That's the thing, I don't think the BBC show was what helped us take off." Ian looked at Theo. "You're huge in Southern USA."

Theo sipped his tea. He hadn't considered his broadcasts to be particularly geotargeted ones. The people of Southern USA must be very hard done by indeed.

"Texas, the Carolinas, half of Florida," Ian continued. "This might explain all those religious messages we've been getting."

"I fucking hate Bible bashers," said Phil.

Ian ignored him and spoke only to Theo. "You can see how your message would connect with them, though, right? We're saying there's another plane of existence with evil forces trying to steal our souls. They're hearing Hell and the Devil."

Theo nodded. He had thought about that.

"I didn't sign up to start talking about God," Phil spat. "I get enough of that shit from the old village deers."

"You're not listening to me," whined Ian. "If Theo says it right, it's the same thing; they just hear it different—"

Phil's fist shot forward and grabbed Ian by the wrist. His knuckles bulged, the flesh blotchy red. Ian let out a high-pitched cry. Behind the bar, Colin remained perfectly calm, taking a sip of ale with one hand, but with the other, out of sight, wrapping his fingers 'round a cricket bat masking-taped to a pipe.

The last six months had been so fast, so intense, all four of them had forgotten they barely knew each other. They knew every single detail of their vast, interconnecting theory on interdimensional vampires controlling the world through a cabal of the global elite, but they knew nothing of Phil's family history of schizophrenia, his two previous convictions for assault, and the collection of World War II paraphernalia in his shed.

"Easy now, boys," Colin said, tightening his grip around the bat. "We're all friends here. Save this for Them out there."

They didn't know that Colin's learning difficulties at school had given him a lifelong gullibility, internalizing what he had been told incorrectly over and over again, that everyone else was smarter than him in every way. The only person who ever told him he was worth anything was his mother, who coincidentally passed away three days before Theo first reached out to book the pub he ran for his Sermon for the Marks.

Ian let out an elongated, frightened whine. They didn't know he had been diagnosed with high-functioning autism, and that while he was very, very good with numbers, he had no comprehension of the impact those numbers had on human people. Nor that the previous year, he had been cruelly spurned and mocked by a woman in the sales department of the IT consultancy firm for which he worked, after finally working up the courage to ask her out.

Phil's grip didn't relax. "I'm hearing you just fine, mate," he said to Ian. "And I'm saying I don't do God shit."

And they didn't know Theo had spent the first thirteen years of his life raised in a fringe Orthodox branch of Christianity.

"If these people are listening, they deserve to be spoken to," said Theo dreamily.

The calmness in Theo's voice soothed Phil. He slowly released Ian's hand. A pale mark remained bound around his wrist, a reminder that no matter how good Ian was with computers, Phil could still beat him to a pulp.

Theo raised his mug of tea again. Ian, Phil, and Colin took hold of their own drinks, hovering them at their chests in anticipation. Ian's hand was trembling, knocking the ice in his drink sharply against his glass.

"Believers," Theo said. "We're going to America."

THEN

Every session with Subject 88 was like the next episode of a trashy science fiction podcast. Audrey was left every week with cliffhanger questions. His vast, interconnecting conspiracy had more twists and turns than the most densely plotted political thrillers. Every answer just spun a new web of mysteries. *Same Subject 88 time, same Subject 88 channel!* In comparison, Audrey's other interviewees were as exciting as watching raindrops erode the Eiffel Tower.

She didn't actually believe Subject 88 was communing with his dead brother. That was ridiculous. Instead, she believed she had found the reason *why* he thought he was. She had found the faulty wiring in his brain. Subject 88 was the missing part in her study's puzzle. He was her new Garry. Not a man in his mid-thirties whose mind had stalled at nine years old, but a teenager, wise beyond his age, who could explain worlds.

Problem was, he was an outlier. She couldn't base her whole study's findings on one example. There was a process. A peer-reviewed, years-long, male-dominated process.

Copernicus didn't do that, she thought. The Earth was the center of the universe for a millennium before he trotted in. How many great ideas had been lost to time's cluttered cupboards? Great leaps forward needed equally great leaps in belief. What was it her grandfather once told her? Belief is just an idea with the parts missing. She'd fill the rest in later.

First, she just had to get people to listen. Then minds would be changed. Lives would be transformed. And she'd be able to shove it in Stephen's face and say, see, this was possible. Our dreams weren't naive. It was you who was wrong and selfish and lazy. *You.*

She'd be celebrated by her university, where she had once been ignored, dismissed as mediocre, put in hack studies. She'd give talks about the importance of real science and tell the story of how she made the single most important discovery of a generation. Dr. Worthington would sit at the back of the hall telling people he trained her, and she would let him say that because, by then, she would be a far better person who could let go of deep underlying personal vendettas.

And, most importantly, she could really help Subject 88. Help him understand his condition and, hopefully, make him see his own brain was working against him. She could fix him.

She could fix everyone.

"You said a few weeks ago that, at first, you only believed in more science-based theories like"—Audrey inhaled—"that New Zealand isn't real. How did that evolve the more you … studied?"

"I still believe in science-based theories, yes."

"I mean, do you now believe in non-science-based theories too?"

Subject 88 considered the question.

"I don't not believe in them."

"How do you mean?"

"Speaking to Benny, it's made me question what else could be real."

Audrey had been carefully laying this trap for weeks. She had established rapport, dismantled defenses, and built trust. She had softened Subject 88 enough to challenge him on his most sensitive subject, and for him not to break into pieces.

"Correct me if I'm wrong, but you didn't 'speak' to your brother. You heard him. He didn't hear you."

Audrey waited, her shoulders bunched with tension, to see if it happened again. To see if her theory was correct. That it didn't actually matter how much you told Earth it wasn't the center of the universe, it wouldn't listen because it thought it was. It *couldn't* listen because, at the end of the day, it was a giant ball of rock.

Subject 88 blinked. "He told me he was trapped and they were draining him."

"That's not what I asked. I asked if he heard *you* speak back to *him*. Because right now"—she braced herself for the confrontational diagnosis—"you could just be hearing what you want to hear."

Subject 88's head leaned forward, his left ear slightly cocked toward her, his face strained like they had a bad connection.

"Sorry, I didn't quite catch that."

He didn't hear me, she thought.

"I said, 'you're hearing things.'"

Subject 88 nodded, doing his best to answer a question he never heard. "Yes, I think the interdimensional vampires are coming for us next."

He actually didn't hear me!

He smiled politely, like Audrey's grandad had smiled and nodded when he'd been 'round for Sunday roasts, despite his hearing aid accidentally having been switched off. Hours, *hours*, he'd sit there like that, pleasantly, not wanting to cause a fuss, content to just smile and nod and smile and nod and be there with his family because he saw in his daughter and granddaughter the best parts of his wife who had passed and left him alone. Both good men who couldn't hear the world around them.

"What else has it made you question?"

"I've always been interested in interdimensional travel, so I decided to look into that first. I developed some theories based on what I read."

"And where did you do this research?"

"On the internet."

"Did you research any peer-reviewed scientific journals?"

Subject 88 strained his ear again, then answered a different question. "My leading theory for the interdimensional hypothesis was that the moment Benny died, his consciousness was stolen by beings in another reality."

Theo flicked his eyes at the window and back. He leaned forward. "You said I can trust you. Do you really mean it?"

Audrey's pulse quickened. *No.*

"Absolutely."

Theo took a deep breath and then revealed how the world really worked.

THE DAWN OF TIME

Long before humans evolved, long before life on Earth, long before the Multiverse exploded into being, all of existence was a black, crushing Darkness. There were no worlds. There were no people. There was no *life*. The infinite Darkness was full of emptiness ...

(apart from one glowing, atom-sized ball.)

The emptiness raged against the ball. It galed and screamed hoarsely into the night. Perhaps the ball was proof there had been another eternity before then, a speck of dust from another time. That the Darkness had already smothered a more ancient reality full of dimensions and worlds and races living life after life after life in its all-enveloping night. Maybe the tale of light overwhelming dark, or dark overwhelming light, isn't the straight line our linear-conditioned minds think it is. Maybe it's a madly twirling dance that goes round and round with no beginning and no end.

Or perhaps that atom-sized ball was the start; no one can say.

All we know is that atom-sized ball contained the Multiverse. And it eventually burst.

O

The Big Bangs signaled a new Epoch of Light. The ball exploded, firing the infinity within at the endless black. The original atom bomb. A chain reaction of elemental building blocks colliding with elemental building blocks began, creating planets, stars, dimensions. In short, all of existence.

Perhaps this was the first time that had ever happened. Perhaps it had played out so many times already; the Gods barely shrugged.

I'm not saying there are or aren't Gods, just that if this happened, they would be rather bored of it by now.

But just how the Light can never truly be extinguished, neither can the Dark be fully shone away. Life, inevitably, casts a long shadow. And like the atom-sized ball that endured, a morsel of original Darkness trespassed into this new bright realm.

The black spot took its time. Stars were born and burned out before anyone even noticed it. Darkness, by definition, is the opposite to Light. Light can burst into a billion brilliant suns in an instant. The flick of a switch, the catch of a match, the explosion of the Big Bangs. But the Dark spreads slowly. It creeps up on you. It *drains* you.

The slither of Black that snuck into the Light bred in dimensions hidden from the sun. It multiplied and evolved, outliving entire alien civilizations, entire galaxies of stars. It developed claws to hold you down with. It gave itself mass to sit heavy on your chest. It reared fangs to pierce your supple flesh.

The Black became a life of its own: a bloodthirsty race of interdimensional predators called the Na'fier.

The Na'fier leeched entire dimensions of life, plunging worlds into perpetual night. They devoured trillions of races. And when those realms are as empty as the Darkness from which they came, they begin to gnaw and bite at the spaces between atoms, ripping holes into adjacent dimensions for them to plunder anew. They have rampaged through realities, tirelessly, hungrily, until there is only one left.

We are all that remains between the Na'fier and the End of the Worlds.

It takes millennia to erode the barriers between realities enough to open a portal. This is called quantum wall diffusion theory, which is very established. The Na'fier finished off the rest of the Multiverse millions of years ago and have been prying at our walls ever since. They've grown very, very hungry.

Civilizations recorded throughout history, and probably those history ignores too, realized this for themselves, and have tried to warn us against the invasion. Stories are embedded in cultures across the world of dark creatures that live in the night. The blood-drinking Lilitu of ancient Mesopotamia. The ghouls of Arabia. The Goddess Sekhmet of Egypt.

We know them by their more modern, Eastern European name: vampyres.

But on July 13th, 1985, the time for warnings had passed. The Na'fier finally broke through in Ethiopia, causing the deaths of entire villages. They were here. And you know what else happened on that date ...

This led to the formation of *The Ten Men*, the secret committee that actually runs the world, currently made up of heads of state, powerful CEOs, and the rapper Jay-Z. They took the only action the '80s knew how. They brokered a business relationship merger.

In return for *The Ten Men* being instilled as the most powerful people on the planet, the Na'fier were allowed sanctioned raids on rogue or dissident states. These targets would have to be unanimously approved by *The Ten Men*, and often involved removing their enemies or serving their geopolitical agenda.

The Na'fier had one small addendum. They wanted to import the "waste product" of humanity into their Dark Dimensions. In their short-term thinking, seeing ahead decades rather than eternity, *The Ten Men* agreed. They hadn't realized the "waste product" was our eternal souls.

They had brokered a deal with the original Devil.

This is what happened to Benny. His soul, or consciousness, or essence, or whatever you want to call it, was ripped from his body when he died in that car crash. Now he's trapped in an eternal pitch black, being torn asunder by a billion demons. His mind flayed for eternity, filling it with dread and hate. Our dark emotions are used as seasoning for their depraved feast.

The Na'fier had underestimated Benny, though. He is special. He's strong. And he's turned what could've been a meaningless death, just another fuel cell for their everlasting war, into a sacrifice. He used the connection he and I had, our love for each other, to warn me about the Na'fier.

They were never going to stop at just our deceased souls. They want those of the living too. Their feeding is growing their awful power. They will soon rip a hole in time-space so gaping, their endless legions will overwhelm Earth in nanoseconds.

We must stop them. *I* must stop them, to prove Benny's death wasn't for nothing. His death *was* meaningful.

THEN (AGAIN)

Audrey sat, mouth open. The skin on the back of her neck tingled at a sudden chill. The room had become so cold she could see her breath puff in faint clouds before her nose. The heavens through the window bulged with purple bruises. Maybe the sky really wasn't blue. Thunder rumbled past outside. There had been no flash of lightning.

She looked over at the real-time brain scans. Subject 88 believed every word he said. To him, this was truth. She saw a single red dot of activity toward the bottom right of his brain. Then another to its left. Then another. Another. Her eyes followed the red spots like a game of hide-and-seek with a nose-bleeding brother to his auditory cortex slightly over his left eye. They intensified, showed up redder, throbbing. Red dots, red dots everywhere.

They were there because for the entire time Subject 88 was talking, the entire time he had been explaining the history of the Multiverse and the Na'fier and *The Ten Men*, Audrey had been challenging every word. Those people in Ethiopia died because of a famine. Quantum wall diffusion theory is actually from a science-fiction fantasy series called *The Qunt Dynasty*. She had been telling him what really happened in the car crash that killed his brother.

He never consciously heard a single thing she'd said. He was so deep in his story, he couldn't even see the movement of her mouth, the waving of her hands. And each challenge, each question, formed a red dot in Subject 88's brain. Where they should've processed as normal speech, every challenge to his beliefs came through as nonverbal white noise.

He literally couldn't hear her.

CHAPTER 3: LOSING MY RELIGION ... BUT REPLACING IT WITH EQUALLY CONTRIVED BELIEF SYSTEMS: A STUDY OF MEANING IN THE POST-TRUTH AGE

THEN

Audrey stood before the brightest psychology minds of her generation from the counties of Kent, Essex, and East Sussex. From her position in the middle of the stage, their wildly clapping hands and beaming faces all looked the same. Insatiably curious, ambitious, bespectacled. Mostly white. It felt like she was graduating in front of an audience of all the past and future possible versions of her. Graduating from what? She didn't know. All she knew, with a heart-pounding, life-fulfilling certainty, was that she was finally changing the world.

They were supposed to have the Shell Oil Center, a modern and morally compromised building constructed in the venue's gardens. But Audrey's findings had rippled through the Southeast of England, causing such excitement that her talk was moved to the biggest space available: the eight-hundred capacity Trigg Hall, an old auditorium named after the seventeenth-century merchant and occasional slave trader Thomas Trigg.

What's more, she had done all this with an accurate, non-pop-song-punning title.

"If this is as explosive as I'm hearing, Dr. Lowe," Poppy Kettering, the curator of the *Psychology Tomorrow … Today!*

annual conference, had told her, "you should really talk to Daddy."

Poppy Kettering's "Daddy" was Terrance Kettering, the editor of the more respectable *Royal Scientific*. She didn't correct Poppy that she wasn't, yet, a doctor.

Audrey picked up one of the cans of water nestled inside the lectern. *So this is what success feels like*, she thought. *Where your water is in a can.* She pulled the tab open and took a cool, metallic sip to calm her throat. It tasted like the future. One free of single-use, nonrecyclable plastic bottles, over which Audrey reigned supreme.

She nodded, signaling the applause to quieten. She controlled them. It had been five months since her last session with Subject 88. Those months had given her the confidence and belief that she was special. That she could change the world. That Stephen was the human manifestation of "limiting belief." She made a promise to herself that she would make the name *Dr. Audrey Lowe* so impactful (once she got her doctorate), it would live forever in textbooks and biographies and seminars to enraptured sixth-form students.

Audrey adjusted the microphone clipped onto her ear. She waited for the last few claps to fade. The red dot above the autocue focused her attention. The taste of liquid future flowed down her throat, into her stomach, and shot instantly through her limbs and fingertips.

She spoke.

"Aural dyslexia might sound like a new invention, but it is really a discovery of something that has been here all along." Audrey paused for everyone to recognize how humble she was being. "Just how Copernicus didn't invent the sun at the center of our solar system, I haven't invented aural dyslexia.

I have simply uncovered the root cause of one of the most pressing issues of our day: Why aren't people listening to each other?"

The crowd erupted in applause. The middle-class academics agreed passionately that people weren't listening to them.

"At the risk of telling a group of Freudians how to love their mothers ..." The audience chuckled warmly. Audrey had read it was important to disarm one's audience with a joke early on. "The most effective way I've found to illustrate aural dyslexia, visually, is using the classic Invisible Gorilla experiment footage."

Audrey stepped to one side of the stage as the video began. It opened on an instruction:

Count how many times the players wearing white pass the basketball.

A thirty-second scene played of six people, three wearing white, three wearing black, passing two basketballs between them.

How many passes did you count? read the next text card.

The correct answer is fifteen passes.

Audrey heard the audience murmur happily. They knew what was coming next.

But did you see the gorilla?

Someone in the crowd exclaimed, "Don't be ridiculous!" Audrey found it comforting that after three decades, the gorilla trick still got people. She dreamt fleetingly of her own experiments still inspiring students thirty, fifty, a hundred years on.

The video rewound itself to the beginning. In clear view, a person wearing a gorilla costume walked into the center of the basketball-passing circle, turned to face the camera, pounded its chest, and then walked off.

The spotlight returned to Audrey.

"Over fifty percent of people completely miss the gorilla, because they're so focused on counting the basketball passes. What's more, even after you've told the subjects about the gorilla, they are certain they couldn't have missed something so obvious.

"This is visual selective attention. Aural dyslexia is that ... for the ears. We *trust* what we see. We *trust* what we hear. In short, we trust our perceptions.

"But what happens if a head injury, which can be very slight—say, hitting your head on an open cupboard door—what if that bump changes the entire way you perceive the world?"

She stepped back again for her next clip. "This is Subject 88."

"Heaven has been taken over by the Devil, and his demon hordes are infiltrating our governments," Theo explained. He wore his smartest shirt and green cardigan for his highest-profile appearance yet, Top Bro's *BroScussion* podcast. With Ian's help, he had packaged the Na'fier invasion threat into a version that would resonate more strongly with his American followers.

Top Bro stared into Theo's eyes. "That's the problem with you Brits. You could say anything in that accent and I'd believe you."

"Well, listen to the content of what he's actually saying, then!" said the TV scientist Maximillian Pound, thumping a scrawny fist on the large wooden desk they sat around. Top Bro had cut down a tree from the vast forest behind his compound, carried it three miles back on his shoulder, and had then carved it into a rustic table for his man-cave-inspired studio.

"Can you not hit the desk, please, Max?" Top Bro said, being very protective of nature when he wasn't hunting it. His brow was a permanent straight line etched halfway down his face. The rest of his features were squashed underneath. He was heavily muscular, with a shaved head and sandpaper beard.

When he listened to you, it felt like he was going to hit you. Theo saw a lot of Phil in him. He knew neither were violent men. They were misunderstood because of their resting angry faces.

Top Bro carefully adjusted a glowing, red plastic Buddha toy that Maximillian Pound had knocked out of position. "And stop interrupting Theo. When you talk over him, it's bad audio, not to mention bad manners."

Maximillian Pound was a respected physics professor at MIT who had found fame telling religious fundamentalists how wrong they were. He had written *The New York Times* best sellers *The Militant Atheist's Ten Commandments* and *Does the Pope Sermon in the Woods?* along with the popular children's series *Derek the Dinosaur That Definitely Existed*. Theo had been watching Maximillian Pound's videos for years and had been excited to meet him. He was happy to find he was just as gracious and intelligent in real life.

"This man is speaking nonsense of the highest order," Pound said, interrupting Top Bro. "He is a danger to science, a danger to rational thought, and a danger to the truth."

Top Bro's jaw jutted out. *Now* he looked like he was going to hit someone.

Maximillian Pound slinked back in his seat, his arms folded like a straitjacket to stop him leaning forward and interrupting again. Top Bro nodded to Theo that it was safe to continue.

Theo swallowed. Every American he'd encountered so far had been welcoming, courteous, and very interested in him preaching some kind of Christian End of Days. Three thousand nine hundred and sixty-two people had attended his first speaking date in the country. CNN reported attendance as slightly over one thousand. Fox News claimed six and a half. It had prompted a fierce debate, which had to be settled the only way the nation appeared to know how these days. On an episode of Top Bro's *BroScussion* podcast.

Ian had told Theo his own livestream figures of eighty thousand were very respectable. Theo glanced at the ticker for Bro's podcast. It read 4,448,988.

"The Na'fier are an ancient and proud race of interdimensional vampires. They have their own strict laws and customs. They are a caste-based society, with different orders and classes of vampires. They have ravaged and conquered the infinite realms but one: ours.

"Their worlds, their *dimensions*, I should say, are nothing like our Earth, though. To imagine it would be like trying to explain a three-dimensional object to a drawing in a comic book. First, they would have no comprehension of what three dimensions are, and secondly, they're inanimate objects. They wouldn't hear you anyway."

Top Bro chuckled warmly. "That makes it very clear in my head. Please tell us more about how we fit into this."

Maximillian Pound shook his head violently.

"Make no mistake about it, we are the last race standing between the Na'fier and the total blackout of the universe. That's their ultimate purpose, to extinguish all light from existence to reestablish the perpetual night from which they spawned. To do that, they need fuel. That's us. They have been able to partly feed off our living souls by making tiny tears between atoms into our universe, which is where I think a lot of mental health issues come from. But it's much worse when we die. They are able to take the entire soul and use that as a battery."

"Goddamn! And what are the so-called 'people in charge' doing about this?"

"They're working with them. They negotiated a shortsighted deal on July 13th, 1985, following a Na'fier incursion off the coast of Africa. They agreed to give the Na'fier mining rights to all humanity's souls once their corporeal bodies had expired."

Top Bro's brow compressed in concentration. "Why do I know that date?"

Maximillian Pound scowled. "It was the first Live Aid concerts for world hunger."

Theo shook his head. "If only it was our world's hunger. Sometime in 1982, the Na'fier punctured through their dimension into ours using quantum wall diffusion." Theo acknowledged Maximillian Pound with a nod, a fellow man of science. "They ravaged Ethiopia in a series of scouting raids, gathering intel on our world before they staged an invasion."

Maximillian Pound pressed his fingers into his eyes. "Those people died because of a famine."

"You're exactly right, because the Na'fier scouting force was draining that country of life. The Darkness would raid entire villages at a time, ripping those poor people's souls from their bodies, and then dragging them back to the Dark Dimensions for an eternal feast.

"The Live Aid concerts were a diversion. The money never went back to Ethiopia; it went to fund interdimensional defense measures off the coast of Australia, preparing our world for the final war of Light versus Dark when it inevitably arrives at our doorstep."

Top Bro had pushed himself back from his microphone, to better take this all in. His brow had lifted to where his hairline was once drawn. He was now Top Brow.

He shook his head. "But Bono did a song for it?"

Theo leaned forward and spoke in an urgent whisper. It was broadcast to an audience that, in the last five minutes, had escalated to over ten million.

"Bono was trying to tell us the truth! 'Feed the world'? To who, Top Bro? To who?"

"Son of a bitch ..." Top Bro massaged the top of his head. The skin folded back and forth.

"There are few people in the world I would trust my entire life to," said Theo. "Bono is one of them."

"So we brokered a deal. Why are the Na'fier trying to invade again?"

"It was a deal with the Devil, which I don't count as being worth very much at all. My brother, Benny, has told me—"

"Sorry to interrupt, Theo. But just for the listeners: he tragically passed away about ten years ago, and has since been sending you warnings from the Dark Dimension he's trapped in."

"Exactly right, Bro. He has told me they are planning a full-scale invasion, as since that deal was brokered, they need more fuel. And them draining fully living souls is far more nutritious than the current arrangement of the souls of the deceased."

"That makes sense. It's like they're living next to the biggest pizza restaurant in the world, and they can only get the crusts."

"I like the crusts."

"I mean, yeah, who doesn't like the crusts? A little bit of cheese in them. Stuff it up. And dip them in garlic-and-herb sauce. Oh yeah. That's heaven. But you want the full slice, you know?"

"I like all of the pizza," confirmed Theo.

"So who's trying to stop this? Surely not all of the people in the so-called government are evil."

"I don't think anyone is really truly evil, Top Bro. I just think they've either fallen on hard times, or they don't fully understand something. Thankfully, we've uncovered that efforts are underway to combat an impending Na'fier invasion. But it's going to take everything this planet has got to defend itself."

"How are they preparing?"

"I can't go into it, because it might compromise certain tactical advantages. But I'll just say this ... New Zealand isn't what you think it is."

"Where they shot the *Harry Potter* movies?"

"*Lord of the Rings*," Maximillian Pound muttered into the microphone, his head in his hands.

"One of the most interesting things I've been thinking about since I came to America," said Theo, "is how all this ties into religion, which we believe is why our message is resonating so strongly with your people."

"It sure is. It's all me and my buddies talk about."

"The Na'fier, how they're organized, how they have the caste-and-order system, it is incredibly similar to the description of Heaven, with how the angels are organized."

"You're right!"

"And if way, way back, millennia ago, before what we consider to be ancient Egypt, maybe the Na'fier were able to break through then. Maybe they briefly opened a portal in the sky, which could be where the original idea of an afterlife came from."

"You're saying the Na'fier's dimension could have been mistaken for Heaven? Which would make here ..."

"Hell," said Maximillian Pound.

"I asked you politely to stop interrupting, Max."

Maximillian spoke as calmly as he could. "I have a duty to myself, to the audience listening right now, and to science: this is a fantasy. You are all distracted by a made-up fiction. Can't you see the reason why your Na'fier lore is so similar to the Christian faith's?"

Theo pressed the headphone cans firmly onto his ears so he didn't miss what Maximillian Pound was trying to help him with.

"It's because you have most likely absorbed the stories of Christianity unconsciously and are now regurgitating them as a science fiction story!"

Top Bro's brow tightened, making it drop half an inch farther down his face.

"What does that matter?" said Bro. "It's chicken and egg. It doesn't matter which came first. We know they're there."

"Only if the chicken and the egg never actually existed! I'm saying Theo's insane conspiracy theory and the founding myths of religion are equally fantastical. In fact, I must admit the only service you are providing this world, Theo, is that you are showing how ridiculous any large overarching conspiracy theory or religion is, simply by holding such an absurd belief and tricking so many people to buy it."

Theo was deeply touched by Maximillian Pound saying he was doing a great service to this world. "Thank you very much," he said.

"Not a compliment."

Theo continued: "I always believed the point of science was to question everything to get to the truth. You have helped me so much with that, Maximillian Pound."

"You have misunderstood everything I stand for."

"Unfortunately, what I've found traveling around your fine country, and through talking to a lot of very interesting individuals, is that a lot of people believe science doesn't seem that interested in the truth anymore. They feel it's just another version of groupthink that believes it has found the answers, and refuses to interrogate deeper into the real reason why the world isn't working for them. It's the same dangerous tribalism that you see at football games, political parties or"— Theo gestured to Top Bro, referencing a point the host had made earlier—"university lecturers."

"Oh great, here we go," said Maximillian Pound, his arms erupting outward, bursting from his self-inflicted straitjacket, slamming down on the desk. "Let's all dunk on my colleagues. What are you going to say next? The postmodernists have gotten out of hand? That we're cooking up terrifying new gender labels in our evil laboratory?"

"That isn't what Theo's saying, Max," said Top Bro. "He's actually raising a good point. I think a lot of us are feeling it right now; certainly I am. So-called scientists these days are making us all feel stupid."

"Well, then read a fucking book," said Maximillian Pound.

Theo was very pleased with this productive consensus. He glanced over at the live chat to see whether people agreed.

What an elitist asshole! I read books all the time - AllWorkNo-Play_0.

Right, because everyone gets their information from "books" these days. It's called the Internet, Maximillian Crap. You're on it right now! - DropOutGetHigh.

I hope Maximillian Pound gets cancer - PhilMeUpButtercup95.

"This is what I'm talking about," Top Bro said. "The so-called great science ambassadors on TV, or with their own podcasts, they're always trying to get people in with the mystery. Wow, this star is a gazillion million miles away. What is it like over there? Look here, there's some new substance that is made a fraction of a second after the start of the universe."

"Those are the most exciting questions of our existence!" cried Maximillian Pound.

"Yeah, but not the *only* questions. That's what I'm saying: everyone in science preaches the importance of questions. But only the right kind of questions that aren't actually any use to the common man. So when someone here like Theo Papadopoulos comes along and disrupts that, the whole community makes a, and I hate to say this, a very *unscientific* agenda against him."

"He's not talking about new elements or dinosaurs, *Bro*. He's talking about world-controlling organizations, that the Eiffel Tower went missing between 1945 and 1954—"

"Damn Hitler," Theo muttered under his breath.

"—and that we're being preyed upon by an eternal race of interdimensional demon vampires."

Top Bro punched his fist knuckles down into the wood. "And what I'm saying is you can't just shut that down. You need to have conversations. You need to listen. You beat ideas with better ideas."

"My ideas *are* better ideas!" Maximillian Pound pointed a cardiganed arm at Theo. "His ideas just sound more exciting. How can I get people to focus on how amazing the structure of deoxyribonucleic acid is or the writing of Hemingway when he's distracting everyone with a two-hundred-million-dollar CGI-laden meaningless blockbuster?"

Theo watched Maximillian's passion in awe. He glanced at the comments feed.

Maximillian Jones should just marry a book. - GymBeasting PT9.

What's dexy's ribbed nuke acid? some kinda lube? - BroBrogan.

tbf fast & furious is better than hemminggay. - Rock4Prez.

Maximillian Pound composed himself. He tugged on the sleeves of his pale green cardigan so they reached his wrists. He placed his palms on the tree-felled table, trying to hold on to a reality no one agreed on.

"I'm sorry, I'm sorry," Maximillian Pound said. His face drooped in regret. "I'm sorry you live in a world that's made you feel stupid. But that is a price of progress. You cannot possibly understand everything anymore. No one can." He picked up his smart phone and waved it, demoralized, by his head. "I don't know how this works. But I know someone else does. I *trust* someone else to know. That's how our society functions." He turned to Theo. "Is that it? Is that why you feel like you have to spread such crackpot theories?" The eyes of Maximillian Pound widened, hoping for their own understanding. "That you've lost your trust?"

"I trust you," answered Theo.

Maximillian Pound put his head in his hands. "No, you don't. You enjoy me. That's not the same as trust."

Theo leaned forward to the microphone, hoping to help Maximillian Pound understand. He seemed so upset that he couldn't quite grasp something.

"You might look around you and see lightbulbs and the internet and smart phones. You see the marvels of modern science. You see the world created by a belief system you trust."

"Science isn't a belief system, it's an empirical building—"

Top Bro covered Maximillian's microphone with his meaty paw. Maximillian took the hint and stopped talking.

"You see the marvels of modern science," Theo continued. "You *trust* in the science. But when I look around me, all I see are jobs being replaced by computers. I hear people telling me over and over again 'I don't have any meaning anymore. I just have apps.' And I *feel* my brother, my own brother, being painfully drained of a soul because the so-called people in charge cut a short-term deal to save their own lives.

"I don't see a world that's working. You ask me for proof. I say to you, prove yourself."

THEN

Audrey entered her dressing room to more applause. It was just one person clapping. She punched the air in victory anyway.

"Did you see me out there, Stephen?" He passed Audrey a glass teeming with wine. Her hands trembled with surplus adrenaline. She didn't spill a drop. "I TED Talked the shit out of them."

Stephen's hand caught her by surprise. It was resting on her shoulder. Over the years, affection had given way to routine. *Breakfast, lectures, lunch, lectures, pub, binge watch, bed.* This tender gesture yanked her back to the kitchen floor nights they shared in someone else's student halls, dreaming how they'd change the world.

He stroked her cheek with his thumb.

"I'm proud of you, Audrey."

Stephen's hand gently cupped her face as the muffled opening chords of Rick Astley's "Never Gonna Give You Up" played through the walls. Dr. Samuel Worthington was taking the stage for his talk on methamphetamine addiction.

The surprise of Stephen's uncharacteristic sincerity passed. Audrey became awkward and self-conscious. She sipped her wine. It suddenly tasted synthetically sweet. She gave Stephen a playful shove away from her.

"And I'm proud of you too, Stephen," she said in a Scottish accent. "Like they say, behind every mediocre man is an amazing woman struggling to publish a groundbreaking psychology paper."

She hadn't intended to be so mean. In her head, it was a play on the cliche, not an accurate summary of what had befallen their relationship. The adrenaline and the wine was like mixing ethanol with absinthe. Maybe she should go watch some of Worthington's talk on addiction.

Stephen turned his back toward her. She could hear the *glug glug glug*, nearing the bottom of the bottle, as he refilled his own glass. He twisted back around and topped her up. She hadn't noticed she was already two-thirds gone.

"Maybe behind every mediocre man is actually a genius grandma."

Audrey drank thirstily. Gulped. "And how's that?"

"Because my gran discovered your aural dyslexia years ago." He leaned into her ear and pronounced every syllable as sharp as a paper cut. "It's called se-lec-tive hear-ing."

That was more like it. Moments ago, Audrey couldn't bear her fiancé being proud of her. Nasty bickering was their comfort setting, foreplay to a sex that had long dried up. His undermining her achievement gave her a deliciously shameful thrill.

"Because no informally recognized personality trait has ever turned out to be a genuine medical condition," she pointed out, her voice dripping with sarcasm. "There's never been some teacher or parent going 'Stephen's a bit slow and can't focus properly in class, isn't he?' And later on, boom, ADHD and dyslexia come along, helping the people afflicted to manage those symptoms."

Stephen leapt on her as soon as she finished, his accent, as statistically trustworthy as it was, thick with irony. "Because psychologists and pharmaceutical industries never create conditions to keep their jobs and medicines in business? How many bored, frustrated kids in class, that really just had crappy teachers or neglectful parents, suddenly got labeled with a disorder?"

"Speaking from experience of your own classroom there?" She threw her hands up in mock delight. "Yay, Mr. Pratt is here to teach us how we shouldn't use our imagination. I've done my research. It's being peer-reviewed. Aural dyslexia is a real condition. It's not people's fault they're conspiracy theorists."

"Maybe not every part of everyday life needs to be diagnosed, Audrey. Maybe people with selective hearing don't have a mental condition. Maybe they're just arseholes."

She stepped toward him, their mouths inches from each other. "Yeah, maybe they are, Stephen." She could feel his breath on her face. "Maybe they are."

They searched each other's eyes, trying to find the arsehole. Audrey broke their stare and turned to top up her glass.

"How do you expect to ever heal the world if you dismiss people so easily?" she said with her back to him. "You disagree with them, so you refuse to engage. I'm telling you, what I've found is going to change that. We're all going to reevaluate the way we interact as a society once I've gone mainstream. It's like deaf people being removed from communities. That's *wrong.*" She was quite drunk now. Her *Psychology Tomorrow ... Today!* talk adrenaline high had a long tail. "We need communities to stay together and celebrate our differences. These people shouldn't be shunned. We need to show everyone the gorilla in the room. They should be talked to, *listened to*, for Christ's sake, and—"

"Told they're wrong?"

Stephen had become eerily calm, his body still, his voice lowered. He would do this on the rare occasions he was about to win. He knew he was the right kind of prick to pop her balloon.

"Because doesn't your aural dyslexia theory suppose there is a 'right' way to think?"

Oh no.

Audrey lost her balance. Her head thick with Rioja, she saw herself. Her life. Her future if she carried on like this with Stephen. Her stomach dilated, a pupil looking inward at an immense emptiness, where, in that moment, she truly understood the black and vast darkness Subject 88 was fighting.

She grabbed hold of the back of the sofa to steady herself. "No, no. Of course there's no *right* way to think."

"You're essentially putting the framework in place to diagnose anyone who doesn't agree with you as mentally ill."

"I'm saying they've suffered physical brain trauma."

"Same thing. You're not honestly rejecting their stupid ideas outright, like I am. You're being far more snide about it. You're just putting another label on them and plastering over their lips to keep their mouths shut."

Audrey was shaking her head. That wasn't what she was trying to do. She was just trying to show everyone the gorilla in the room.

NOW

Phil's teeth glinted in the moonlight. He huddled Theo, Colin, and Ian around him in the endless dark behind a biker's bar, a long way out of town, and a long, long way from home.

He had a gun.

"Want to see me shoot it?" he asked Theo.

"Where did you get it?"

Phil's thumb caressed the handle. "One of the bikers in there." He gestured at the bar. The muffled sound of music and chatter drifted through the empty night's air. "They all listen to you."

Theo had found the bikers very welcoming, like almost everyone he had met in America. He had put it down to the famous Southern hospitality. They had joked about his tea as they all drank whiskey. Perhaps this weaponized gift was just one of their customs.

Still. The gun made him feel slightly uneasy.

But he had never seen one shot, live in person. As per his own philosophy, he should see the evidence for himself. Otherwise, how would he know if guns really were dangerous?

"Yes," he said.

Phil rubbed the gun handle faster. "Yes what, chief?"

"I want to see you shoot it."

Phil hopped in excitement. "I won't let you down, chief." He shoved the weapon haphazardly in his belt to free both hands. He embraced Theo strongly and whispered in his ear, "You've given me so much. I want to show you what I can give in return."

Theo hugged him back and nodded into his shoulder. It showed the power of his message. An angry, directionless man like Phil had been transformed on their shared mission to unite the world to fight for peace. To *save* the world.

Phil tore himself from their embrace, pointing at something behind Theo. He leapt forward and began stomping on the earth.

"Fucking—" *CRUNCH* "—spying—" *CRUNCH* "—communist—" *CRUNCH* "—bastards—" *CRUNCH*.

The last *crunch* hung in the air like a broken neck. Phil turned around to face them, his cheeks red from crunching rage. He motioned to the darkened, wet patch of ground where he'd been stomping.

"Snail," he said.

He turned and strode into the night. Each construction boot step billowed a cloud of unsettled dust. Each step another construction boot down a certain path.

"I wish he still had his high-vis jacket on," Ian whispered to Theo, his voice even higher than usual. "He'd be easier to keep track of then. He's got a gun, for God's sake. A gun!" He continued to whisper, but Theo could no longer hear him.

Phil marched into the Arizona desert. He stopped fifteen feet away. The back of his light blue jeans still reflected the fluorescent striplight glow of the bar. He raised his right arm as though the gun were a part of it and fixed its aim onto the dark horizon.

"We need a tin can or something," Colin said, holding a weak American beer in his hand. Volume can compensate for strength, though, and he'd drunk so many he was swaying side to side in the warm breeze. "He needs a tin can on top of a fence post to shoot, like they do in the movies." He called out to Phil. "There's nothing there, mate. What you aiming at?"

Phil stared into the night. "Them," he said, his breath fogging in the air despite its mildness.

He fired the gun. The bullet went one way, Phil's thumb went the other.

He never knew how to wield a gun safely. He held it like how a child would make a finger gun, index finger pointed out, three fingers wrapped round the handle, a thumb up in the air for the trigger. The chamber's recoil had snapped the latter clean off. He howled and cursed into the night, leaving a bloody red trail in the desert dust, as he tried to find his severed digit. All while the bar emptied of laughing leather-clad men, only making him angrier at the world.

Theo followed the red dots on the ground.

Benny! Coming to find you, ready or not!

Phil looked cross-eyed at the place where his thumb used to be.

"I ... my ..."

He fainted backward. Ian sprinted toward him, as fast as his waddling legs would waddle him. He caught Phil in his arms and cradled his head.

"Help!" Ian yelped to the bikers.

Colin drunkenly staggered over, saw Phil's freshly aero-dynamic hand, and projectile vomited out onto America's glorious, epic plains.

A biker swaggered over. He introduced himself as Rusty Knucks.

"Mr. Knucks, we can't use your healthcare system," Ian panted. He fumbled out his inhaler and took a hit. He was now supporting all of Phil with just one arm. He was stronger than he knew.

"You folks not got insurance?"

"No, of course not," Ian shrieked. "The US healthcare system is run by the Rockefellers as an organ harvesting scheme."

Rusty Knucks rubbed his wiry black beard flecked with gray. "That it is, I'm afraid." He threw his own thumb over his shoulder. "Doc inside can fix you up."

"Is Doc a doc?"

"Nope. But he's handy with a needle and thread. And scalpel. And a Ruger 10/22 Carbine Semiauto Rimfire Rifle." Rusty Knucks surveyed the surrounding area. "We'll be needing that part of you that's no longer part of you, though."

A howl echoed over the barren dirt, ricocheting off the horizon's darkened, jagged mountains and rising into the chilled expanse of night above them. Phil opened his eyes and pulled Ian close at the monstrous sound.

"Maybe we better leave the digit ... ," Rusty said, angling one big biker's boot to bolt toward the bar.

The blackened panorama shrieked again, closer this time. The four men stared into the abyss, their boots fixed in the dust, when the beast's outline etched itself out in the darkness. It strode toward them, the moonlight filling details in silver and black, to reveal the form ... as Theo.

He held a small object over his head, pointing it defiantly toward the Na'fier realm waiting hungrily above them.

"Believers, I am not one to look for meaning where there could just be coincidence, but this, *this* shows us we are on the right path."

He lowered the object so it was no longer silhouetted by the moon. It was Phil's thumb.

"Benny just gave our mission a thumbs-up."

CHAPTER 4: SUSPICIOUS MINDS ... BUT ONLY OF EVERYONE ELSE: WHY PEOPLE FAIL TO ACKNOWLEDGE SELF-PROJECTED FLAWS IN THEIR CONCLUSIONS

THEN

Maris Piper potatoes, burrata, a bottle of Rioja. Maris Piper potatoes, burrata, a bottle of Rioja. Maris Piper …

Audrey repeated the list in her head like she was a Soviet sleeper agent. She was on a secret mission to get all the items Stephen had forgotten to pick up. She was throwing a celebratory dinner party for herself. She was about to be published.

The *Psychology Tomorrow … Today!* talk had led to Audrey being introduced to Terrance Kettering, the editor in chief of the *Royal Scientific*. He called her work "the most exciting psychology development in two decades, my dear." His journal would publish her paper in four days' time.

That wasn't the only "talk" that had changed her life, though. The night in the greenroom afterward had removed the last lumen of light from her engagement. She had finally spoken aloud Stephen's secret. That he was mediocre and had no imagination. He hadn't looked at her the same since. And, to be honest, neither had she.

Her nose wrinkled at the fruit-and-veg aisle. The baskets overflowed with impossibly yellow bananas and bright red peppers, but the artificially chilled air had the underlying reek of rot. Her eyes ran over green plastic bins of potatoes in all their English variations, like a roll call of the royal family:

King Edward, Duke of York. Large, small, knobbled, spherical, white, purple.

Subject 88.

She stood frozen in shock. On the other side of the potato baskets was her star subject. She hadn't seen him for over a year. His head was still shaved.

"Hello," he said.

He would only be sixteen now, his face still smooth and young. But he was already taller than her, and his eyes had aged in dog years. Still, he had the same polite, warm disposition. It made her ashamed. She broke eye contact.

"Imagine bumping into you here," she replied, trying to keep the guilt from her voice.

"It's our local supermarket."

"I suppose it is."

They stood in silence.

"Well," Audrey said. "I'm very sorry, but I've got a party tonight and I've got to get a few more bits—"

"Is it your birthday?"

"No … it's a celebration party."

"Congratulations."

"Thank you."

"What are you celebrating?"

She straightened, to face the consequences of her actions head-on. "You."

He stood stoically. Unmoved. She wanted to break the silence like someone drowning wanted a gasp of air. "Would you like to come?"

She cursed herself inwardly. Why had she asked?

"I would love to," he said, reaching a hand through the potatoes. "My name is Theo Papadopoulos, by the way."

She shook. "Audrey Lowe," she said.

The red dots all meant the same thing, Theo thought. That you know for sure someone is actually listening to you. They just got bigger.

They had started with the blinking red diodes on Dr. Audrey Lowe's experimental headset. Then the recording light over the lens of *HearRational*'s streaming camera. Top Bro had a snow-globe-sized ON AIR orb in the middle of his podcast desk. *The Tonight Show with Jimmy Holiday*, where he sat now, had a light the size of a shoebox above the greenroom door, the word *LIVE* written white in its red box.

He was collected, walked through dark backstage curtains, and unveiled in front of a studio audience.

The cheers overwhelmed him in their cacophonous din. He searched the middle rows for something, someone to hold on to. He saw Ian, sweating. Phil was cracking his knuckles, reattached digit included. Colin had a pub to run and had gone back to Swanley. A long way from New York City.

In front of him, Jimmy Holiday stood at his desk, his hand outstretched. Theo took it and shook. Jimmy Holiday placed his other hand on top and pressed warmly.

"You've got a lot of fans out there," he said, gesturing to the crowd. They cheered louder. He leaned forward, his lips close to Theo's ear. "You've got a lot of fans back here too," he whispered.

Theo nodded. They sat down.

"What a reaction," Jimmy Holiday shouted, clapping himself. "You're a popular guy!"

"I think it's the truth that's popular," replied Theo.

"Let's get a round of applause for that!"

The audience was already applauding anyway. The Americans never seemed to stop.

"What a few months it's been for you. From wowing crowds down in Texas, then that amazing appearance on Top Bro's show. That's where I first heard you, by the way, and it's when you delivered that awesome catchphrase for the first time." He turned to the audience. "What was it again, folks?"

"Prove Your-Self! Prove Your-Self!" they chanted. One man ripped off his shirt to reveal a vest he'd scribbled *PROVE YOURSELF* on in black marker pen. A young woman pulled up her shirtsleeve and flexed an arm tattoo of Theo's face with *PROVE USELF* written in a speech bubble coming from his mouth. A grandma held a baby above her head like it was Moses's tablets. The baby's bib read *Na'fier Gonna Happen!*— a popular anti-Na'fier slogan a merchandising company had released for him, five percent of all proceeds going to the invasion defense effort.

"It's very humbling," Theo said, smiling. "You Americans are very welcoming."

"Good God, I love your accent." Jimmy Holiday gave him seductive eyes. Theo thought it was interesting how Bro looked like he wanted to hit him, and Jimmy looked like he wanted to sleep with him. Perhaps there wasn't that big a difference.

"Prove yourself, that's your mantra. I love it, I love it!"

Jimmy Holiday leaned forward and mock whispered, "Listen, T-Man. All right if I call you 'T-Man'?"

The audience was sniggering, anticipating a bit.

"T-Man is fine."

Jimmy Holiday looked around, pretending to check that no one could hear him. "Look at me. I'm a schmuck. Sure, I dress great and I have fantastic hair, but deep down I'm a wreck. I chat to famous celebrity after famous celebrity. Leading men and women, politicians, goddamned Olympians with rock-hard abs. It gives a guy confidence issues, you know."

In the last several months, Theo had absorbed how to behave around American audiences and hosts. They loved light joshing, so he emphasized looking up and down Jimmy Holiday's lanky body. "I can see how that would happen."

"I deserve that." He leaned forward even more, his elbows sliding his torso across the desk a ridiculous distance. "So what I want to know is ... how do I prove *myself*?"

Theo thought about it. "Ask questions."

Jimmy Holiday feigned exasperation. "I just did!"

Theo smiled. "I think we define ourselves by the questions we ask. It's constantly interacting with the world around us. Testing ideas, challenging realities. Don't rely on other people to give you the answers. Ask questions until you have an answer that makes sense to you. Then, you will find meaning."

Jimmy Holiday sat back. His hand hovered to his heart. "That's beautiful, man. I wish I could see the world the way you do." He shook it off. "Until then, though, the only question I'll be asking tonight is 'vodka or whiskey?'"

The crowd erupted. They found alcoholism very funny.

"Jimmy needs a drink!" Jimmy Holiday hollered to the crowd. The brass band by the stage played a jazz punchline interlude.

Theo observed Jimmy Holiday. He was very skilled at guiding his audience. Not controlling them, but riding their waves of momentum. He could sense what was coming next. Jimmy Holiday had used a comedic opening to defuse the crowd, creating a safe, happy space for the more serious chat that would follow. He noted to himself to use that in his own work. Listen to your tribe. Go where they want you to go.

"Did you ever think you'd become a modern-day prophet?" Jimmy Holiday asked as the laughter calmed.

"No, never."

"You didn't start out that way?"

"No."

"Tell me. Tell me how you started out."

THEN

"I've got the Rioja. Thanks for nothing, Stephen."

"You're welcome," Stephen called, walking in from the living room at the promise of wine. He stuttered in the hall. "You've also got a schoolboy?"

Theo stood next to Audrey in the front doorway holding four bags for life.

"Yes, Stephen. Please meet Theo Papadopoulos. He was kind enough to help carry all the shopping you didn't do home."

Stephen screwed up his face before he recognized him from the presentation video. His head darted fiercely to Audrey. His eyes bulged, his brow furrowed. A facial expression: *Subject 88?!*

"What are you doing bringing him back here?" Stephen whispered as loud as he could. Audrey pressed shut the kitchen door.

"I bumped into him at the supermarket."

"I fail to see how that explains why Subject 88 is in our house right now. I bumped into a street preacher with a PA system in the park today. I didn't bring him back. Because he's insane."

"Theo isn't insane."

"You want to bring this all up again?"

"As the only person here with a psychology PhD, I'll take your expert opinion on board."

Stephen grabbed her arm. "You don't have a PhD yet." His eyes narrowed. "Is that why he's here?"

Audrey shook Stephen's grip off her. "No, no … honestly, I don't know." She started unpacking the shopping. "He asked me what I was getting Maris Piper potatoes for, and I told him it was for a party to celebrate him."

"You did what?" Stephen slammed his hand on the kitchen counter. "That's a creepy conversation for a twenty-seven-year-old woman to have with a schoolboy in a supermarket, before *bringing the schoolboy back to her house!*"

"Crap." She threw the bag for life on the counter.

"Yeah, you've really screwed up this time, Audrey."

"I have." She looked him in the eyes, defiant. "I forgot the potatoes."

The kitchen door swung open, its little panels of glass rattling against the wall. Audrey walked through with a tumbler of red wine filled to the brim.

Theo sat on the sofa, leafing through an issue of *Psychology Tomorrow*. Audrey took the seat next to him, even though the room had five other randomly assorted chairs for the night's guests.

"That magazine is full of crackpots," she said, taking a long drag of wine.

"Is that where your paper is going, then?" Theo gently joked.

Audrey smirked. "No. I heard, this morning actually. I heard this morning that it's going in the *Royal Scientific*."

Theo smiled blankly back. She felt like she had to explain herself.

"*Psychology Tomorrow* is just pop science. The *Royal Scientific* is the most respected peer-reviewed journal in the country. And they want to publish my paper in there."

She was boasting. It felt good. Whenever she spoke about this to Stephen, she could feel the resentment radiating off him. Theo looked proud of her.

"What's pop science?" he asked.

Audrey waved her hand dismissively at the magazine. "It's just nonsense that people read on the loo. Stuff like the seven personality traits. It's massively oversimplified, or sometimes utter fantasy. No one really takes it seriously."

Theo nodded, obviously not having heard her. The silence between them filled with Audrey's realization of her own pomposity.

NOW

"I was the subject of a science experiment," Theo told Jimmy Holiday. "But they lied to me."

"Now that's something you don't hear every day. What special powers did you get? Flight, super strength, invisibility?"

"I guess you could say it gave me the ability to see through everyone's BS."

The audience applauded and laughed in equal measure.

"So you're saying you were actually part of a science experiment. With needles and special solutions?"

"No," Theo said. "With questions. It was to look at my mind."

"And they lied to you?"

"They told me it was to investigate paranormal events through a scientific lens. I had just lost my brother in a car accident."

"I'm so sorry."

"I appreciate that, thank you. Benny had just died. It was no one's fault. My dad was driving him to swimming lessons, but he lost control of the car. There was black ice on the road. He'd put the winter tires on; he obsessed over that car. He checked it every Sunday morning while he washed it, no matter the weather."

"That must've been very tough on you."

"It was, but it was tougher for my dad. He blamed himself. He loved that car."

Jimmy Holiday's face hung. The audience shifted uncomfortably.

"That was a bad joke, sorry. You kind of come up with bad jokes like that for situations like these. For all of you, this is the first time you're hearing it. But for me, I've been telling this story over and over since I was thirteen. You come up with new little spots to amuse yourself, to show there's actually nothing wrong with you."

"Like a stand-up routine?"

"Yeah, pretty similar, I guess. Just with the aim of emotionally distancing yourself."

"Hey, show me a stand-up comedian, and I'll show you someone who's trying to emotionally distance themself."

The crowd chuckled warmly. The candid, confessional tone was far different from the usual polished, orchestrated anecdotes of late-night TV.

"I missed Benny a lot, but even in the year after he passed, I never believed in vampires. I never even believed in Father Christmas."

"Excuse me, Theo. Santa Claus is most definitely real."

"I don't rule anything out, anymore." Theo smiled. "Then one night, about a year after Benny died, I see an advert online. Just one of those little square pictures next to an article, and it said, 'Do you feel drained?'"

"Do you feel drained?" Jimmy Holiday echoed.

"Yeah. I'd heard of sinks being drained. Or wounds, maybe. But I'd never thought of a whole person being drained. I thought the correct word would be 'burned out.'"

"The correct word here might be 'mad.'"

The audience chuckled.

"Maybe. I clicked through and it had more details. The headline read: 'Applicants wanted for scientific study into supernatural encounters.' And then it continued below—"

FARTHER BACK THEN

Have you experienced an event you can't explain?

Are you doubting the fundamental building blocks of life?

UFOs?

Political conspiracies?

The water erosion of the Eiffel Tower?

If so, we NEED to hear from YOU. We want to learn from you and understand these incredible events.

Theo stood up with such force, his desk chair wheeled back and knocked into the bed behind him. He didn't hear the clatter. Neither did his parents, who had not been listening for a while.

He was overridden with a need, a compulsion. He walked out his room, across the landing, past Benny's room, which had been stripped, redecorated, completely overwritten, like he had never existed at all. Even his smell had been eradicated, replaced with the aroma of synthetic new plywood and flatpack furniture plastic packaging.

He relied on his ears to pick up his mother and father blindly watching television downstairs. They'd think the creaks of his feet on the floorboards was him going to the bathroom. He opened the toilet door, closed it, but never went in. An aural diversion. Then he gently, silently, but quickly opened his parents' bedroom door. A strange place, like the teachers' room, where he always suspected they had other interests and personalities beyond being Mum and Dad.

He walked hurriedly to their wardrobe and soundlessly opened its doors. He parted his mother's hanging clothes and lifted his father's heavy coats, where the ossuary rested lifelessly beneath them.

Theo ran his hands over its mahogany lid. He flinched backward. Despite being wrapped in thermal jackets, the box was as cold as ice, and his breath mysteriously fogged before his eyes.

He grabbed a fistful of waterproof gilet, ready to bury Benny all over again, walk away, and forget he had ever spoken to him from beyond the grave. But his brother needed help. His brother needed him.

Theo rummaged through coat pockets until he found two gloves. They were mismatched and oversized, but he didn't have time for everything to fit perfectly. He touched the ossuary again, his breath misting more the closer he got, and opened the box full of his dead brother's bones.

Theo stared at them for a fraction of a moment that lasted an hour. The curtains weren't yet drawn. Street and moonlight painted the room in black and white. Of all the objects, the skeleton was the whitest; so white it appeared to glow itself. He willed his brother to speak again, to talk to him like they had three months ago. The bones sat there, dead as dead. He reached in, picked up his dead brother's humerus. He expected it to feel smooth. Instead, it was pocked like honeycomb. He held it up to his ear. Nothing.

A sound stirred downstairs. His father getting up to piss. Theo closed the box, closed the wardrobe, closed the bedroom door, and leapt into the bathroom and flushed.

He walked out and passed his bleary-eyed father on the landing. They didn't talk to each other. They hadn't talked to each other for a long time.

Theo sat back down at his desk and read the advert again.

Do you feel drained?

Theo put his hands in the pouch pocket on the front of his hoodie and felt the bone that he'd stolen from his brother's grave. For the first time since Benny died, he didn't feel so alone.

THEN, AND SOMEWHERE
IN THE MIDDLE, AGAIN

"A toast to the happy couple, Audrey and Theo!"

"Stephen!" Audrey slapped Stephen's arm as he sat down at the table. This was no light couple banter. It was heavy, dizzy with red wine. She stood up and steadied herself on the dining room table.

"Thank you so much, all of you, for coming. And thank you to our guest of honor." She did a mock curtsey, nearly slipped, caught herself. "Theo Papadopoulos, of Wilmington College."

"Ah, Wilmington," said Terrance Kettering, editor of the *Royal Scientific*. His tweed blazer hung open over his vast stomach, his glass balancing on the shelf of his gut. He spoke through teeth flecked purple with wine. "A dear friend of mine, Old Winston, went to Wilmington Grammar School too. A fine tradition, young man. You'll be able to talk to him at an Alumni Evening one day."

"I go to Wilmington College, sir," Theo corrected, not wanting to give Old Winston false hope. Students needed either very high entrance exam scores to get into Wilmington Grammar School, or very high-income parents.

"I wouldn't worry, Theo," said Stephen, glaring. "You're going to be famous no matter what school you went to."

"Stephen, stop being such an arse," said Audrey. She looked at Theo. He had started cutting his food.

"You're going to be a big, famous subject of a big, famous study," Stephen continued. Flecks of red spit fell on his freshly shaved chin. "Do you know what that study was?"

"Stephen, would you shut the fuck up—"

"Let me talk, Audrey. It's important he knows why he's going to be famous."

"You don't care about Theo, at all. You're just saying this to antagonize me."

"And you do 'care' about this kid? Exploiting him to make a name for yourself?"

Audrey felt Theo's eyes drift over to her. He smiled.

"Look at me, kid." Theo rested his knife and fork on his plate and faced Stephen. "Do you know what the study was actually for?"

Theo felt embarrassed, as though he'd been caught in his parents' room. He answered Stephen's question as best he understood it.

"The experiments were to collect anecdotal stories of supernatural or extraterrestrial phenomena, to see if there was any trace left on the subjects' brains." He concentrated on speaking as calmly and scientifically as possible, as he was around scientific people. "Like if you had been abducted by aliens, the experiment would see if they had left any physical proof of that in your brain."

"No, it wasn't to see if"—Stephen exaggerated air quotes—"'phenomena' were leaving marks on brain activity." He turned to Terrance. "Can you believe he actually believes that?" He turned back to Theo. "Wrong way 'round, kid. It's to see if your defective brain caused you to imagine a supernatural event."

Theo brought his hands together as he realized what Stephen was saying. "Yes, I believe the supernatural event, in my case, contact with another dimension, did leave some kind of mark on my brain. That's why ever since I've been picking up more and more occurrences."

Stephen stared at him. His anger dissipated as quickly as it came, leaving a dumbfounded, slack-jawed expression on his face. Audrey put her head in her hands, her fingers losing themselves in her long auburn hair.

"My God ... ," Stephen said. "It's true. Aural dyslexia. You really don't hear what doesn't agree with you."

"To be fair, Stephen," said Audrey, her chin sunk into her chest, "neither do you."

Theo smiled again. It felt nice that they were finally all on the same page.

THEN

"The applications for this go far beyond understanding the conspiracy theory leaning mind, Audrey," said Terrance Kettering, editor in chief of the *Royal Scientific*. His teeth were no longer purple with last night's wine, but the years and years of dinner parties left a blotchy discoloring around his cheeks. In lieu of a glass, a fountain pen balanced precariously on his gut. Books and academic journals lined the floor-to-ceiling shelves behind him. The vastness of his brain had wall space. "Aural dyslexia could apply to many areas of psychology and sociology."

Audrey felt her chest filling with pride, smothering any remnants of guilt she had for exploiting Theo, for ignoring the problems with Stephen, for not visiting her grandfather enough. Terrance Kettering could be her grandfather now. He was old enough, and he listened to her, supported her. Someone was finally here to realize how great she was.

"I hope you don't mind; I gave a friend a copy outside the peer-review group."

Audrey blushed. "No, not at all."

"He was very excited for the applications to politics. Imagine! All this time we've been having this bipartisan debate, which we believe to be the most pragmatic version of liberal democracy, when, really, nobody can hear each other. It's akin to just seeing who can shout the loudest."

"Maybe we could all start a new society in Surrey and never interact with the other side."

Terrance Kettering laughed a deep, friendly laugh. "If only, Audrey! If only!"

He leaned forward. His chair creaked. The pen remained unmoved on his stomach, elegant and sharp.

"I have one concern, though," he said, dropping his voice. "You have treated me like a mug."

A trapdoor opened in the pit of Audrey's stomach.

"I would—I could never treat you like a mug, Terrance."

He leaned back. The chair didn't creak. Audrey wanted it so desperately to make a sound, a splinter, a strain.

"I'm afraid you have, Audrey. Our peer-review process found no issues with your research; in fact, they were all tremendously excited by the prospect. *I* was tremendously excited too, precisely because the peer reviewers were. That's why I showed it to my friend. Do you think I show every flaw-ridden, speculative, pseudoscientific bollocks that makes its way to me to my very good friend in the Commons?"

Audrey shook her head, her ear striving to hear a creak. If she could get a creak, maybe everything would go back to how it was a few minutes before.

"While your paper passed the peer reviewers, no mean feat, it was brought to my attention through a ..." Terrance paused as he searched for a phrase. "A very passionate separate channel that there was a significant flaw in your process."

"What separate channel? Who s-said this? I-I ... ," Audrey stuttered. She couldn't get her words out. She didn't want to hear this.

"You have performed bad science, Audrey. Very bad, bad science. You deviated from your standardized questions for one subject. A, er ... er ..." He shuffled through the papers on his desk. "Subject 88. You let your interest in his case hijack the rest of the experiment and left out the parts that revealed your influence. You have overemphasized his behavior in the other subjects you've interviewed. Going back over the video interviews, nobody else in your study shows signs of aural dyslexia. They are stubborn, yes. Delusional, practically all of them. But not a single one, other than 88, displays behavior fitting with your newly diagnosed condition."

"That can't be ... I remember." *Subjects 64, 19, 122* ... Unreliable faces flashed through her mind. "I remember the others not hearing too."

"What's more, the child's parents have no recollection of signing a consent form. Without that"—he waved the paper—"all this is invalidated. The only other person in this experiment who had this aural dyslexia you've invented ... is you."

Audrey's heart stopped.

"This is the last four years of my life."

"Maybe that was the problem." Terrance was already returning to his papers. "There's too much of *you* in this."

Audrey's chest was moving up and down, but no air was breathing in. Her lungs were empty. She could feel the individual alveoli crumpling, the branches of bronchioles withering and snapping off.

"You may leave now," said Terrance, not looking up. "You can always make a name with something else," he pondered. Audrey willed for his chair to creak. If she could just hear that sound again, that break, maybe all this would reset.

"What about how researchers project their own conclusions on experiments and ruin the results? Munchausen's research by proxy. Ha!"

Maybe none of this was actually happening.

And that was when she realized ... this is all a *dream*. That is what happens when you spend too much time with delusional people. The delusions rub off on you.

"Good one, Dream Terrance. You nearly had me there."

Dream Terrance's eyebrow arched. "Pardon me?"

Audrey relaxed into her chair, air reinflating her lungs. "This isn't real. This is an anxiety dream. I'm actually in bed right now, the night before we have our meeting."

"I assure you, my dear, this is very unfortunately real."

This was exactly what Dream Terrance would say. Thankfully, she had science on her side.

Audrey remembered that the unconscious had no need for the linearity of time. Lucid dreamers would wake themselves inside their minds by checking a clock twice in quick succession. They would confirm they were asleep if the time randomly jumped, from 12:19 p.m. to 3:03 p.m., for example. Or 9:56 a.m. to 11:28 p.m. She had heard all this on a podcast.

She grabbed the LED clock from Terrance's desk. Two red lights blinked on and off in its center, making a colon separating the hours from the minutes.

"Right now, this clock reads ten forty-three a.m. I'm going to look away, then look back again, and it'll display a totally different time because dream time isn't consistent."

Terrance's other eyebrow arched, underlining his forehead with an angrily confused letter *M*.

She held the clock away from her face, waited a few moments, and looked back. It read 10:44 a.m.

"Okay, that's not enough data. This could still be a dream."

Terrance pressed the intercom on his desk. "Clarissa, would you please be a darling and escort Audrey out? She can't decide whether we're all figments of her imagination."

Audrey stuck to her hypothesis. Because that's how science is done. You have a hypothesis, and you test it. You get results, you test it again. That's good science. She is good at science.

She ran around Terrance's desk, still gripping the clock in her white-knuckled hand. Its power lead clotheslined across the desk, pushing a stack of papers to the floor. She pulled several books from the shelves.

"Okay," she breathlessly explained. "For oneironauts—or 'lucid dreamers'—checking the time is just one way to tell if they're asleep. Another way is looking at the text in a book. I'll open this book, read a part of the page, close it, open it again, and the text will be different. Then we can all agree that I'm dreaming."

"And if it's not?" Terrance growled. He spoke in such a low voice, Audrey could barely hear him.

"Don't worry about that, I'm quite sure I'm dreaming," Audrey laughed. "Because if I'm not, this would ruin my career!" She threw a couple of books across the room with abandon.

"Terrance—" came a woman's voice as the office door opened. A hardback copy of Maximillian Pound's 1,042-page opus *God, No* struck her in the head. She fell backward, pulling the door shut with her.

"Clarissa!" Terrance yelled, standing up. "That is quite enough, young lady," he bellowed, turning toward Audrey.

"Wait," she said, frantically flicking through a book. It was book four in Maximillian Pound's less well-received adult fantasy novel series *Dragon Chasers*. "I need to prove you're not real!" She ran her finger down a page searching for a line, any line, to pull her out.

Terrance pressed a different button on the intercom. "Stanley, please come to my office at once to remove an abusive party."

"Here's one!" Audrey quoted Maximillian Pound. *"And then, he deduced, magicians told lies, the distant land of Academia was a fantasy, and, most of all, dragons could not fly."*

Audrey shut her eyes. When she opened them again, the text would be different. But behind those scrunched-up lids, new images flooded her vision.

She was buying potatoes. She was receiving a standing ovation. She was looking at red dots. She was sitting in a hot car with blood streaming from her nose. She was drinking wine in a first-year dorm room. She was holding her grandfather's crinkled hand in a park.

She opened her eyes and read out loud: *"And, most of all ... dragons could not fly."* The book made a soft *thwump* as it fell to the floor. "But ... that can't be?"

"Time to come with me, miss," came a voice behind her.

Something firm wrapped itself around the top of her arm. The pressure was uncomfortable, but it didn't hurt.

It didn't hurt.

Audrey lunged out of the security guard's grip and snatched the fountain pen from Terrance's hand. She dragged its point across her palm, carving her head line with navy-blue ink. Stanley the security guard disarmed her and tackled her to the ground. Audrey watched the pen roll across the carpet and come to rest at Terrance's light brown brogues. She would never have noticed from up above, but they were speckled with magenta drops. She wondered if it was ink, wine, or blood.

She looked at her palm, and the fleshy flap she'd cut into it. At first, there was no pain. But then the rip in her skin zipped open. Blood oozed out from left to right, darkening as it mixed with the ink. And a sweet, pulsating pain shot up through her arm and made her scream into the ground with a clarity of mind she felt she had never fully had.

"Science lies." Jimmy Holiday shook his head. "Up yours, Mrs. Pinnicky in third grade!" The crowd screamed in delight. Jimmy Holiday motioned for them to quieten. "Sorry if I'm being dumb, but where was the bit where they lied? You said they did an experiment on you, they discovered your brain worked on the right frequency to tap into messages from other dimensions, and then they'd help get your message out to warn the world." Jimmy Holiday gestured to the audience. "Looks to me like those all worked."

Theo smiled as he waited for the audience to settle. "The bit where they lied was when they told me that science was a force for good. To inquire about the world. To entertain all theories and to test them. And when someone, a brilliant and brave scientist called Audrey Lowe, who was the person who discovered me, the first person to ever truly *listen* to me, uncovered the unique way my brain worked, they shut her down. She was about to be published in the most respected scientific journal in the world, and the powers that be canceled her."

Theo looked directly down the lens, instinctively improvising with the multicam setup, an operator's red light popping on, tracking gently toward him on a gliding platform.

"If science was as pure as everyone says it is, I could've warned you all eight years ago when Audrey Lowe first discovered me. Think of all the souls we could've saved if we knew back then what we know now."

Jimmy Holiday shook his head. "It would be immeasurable."

"Science pretends to be a modernizing force. But it's as institutionalized as any other large community groupthink. Science is afraid of new ideas. Its great hypocrisy is that it pretends to want them."

"You truly are a special human being. I am so glad you came on here tonight, to share your gift with the world. But you didn't just come on here to talk on your biggest stage yet; you chose us, *The Tonight Show with Jimmy Holiday*, for the first time ever, to prove you can actually walk the walk. On tonight's episode, you will be communicating with another dimension *live on-air!*"

"Yes, I will."

"But before you do, we have a surprise for you. We, of course, know the great esteem you hold Audrey Lowe in. And for the first time since you were a teenager, we'd like to reunite you both!"

Jimmy Holiday's arm gestured behind Theo. The studio suddenly went blurry, and he realized his eyes had become wet. He could see the audience clapping, their palms beating excitedly against each other, but he couldn't hear them. He could only hear a voice from behind his shoulder.

He turned and saw Audrey standing across from him, the guest sofa between them. Her eyes were wet too. She was mouthing something, but his ears had shut down. She stepped toward him, around the sofa, and they held each other, live, on network TV.

"What a beautiful moment!" Jimmy Holiday yelled over the crowd. "For the first time in almost ten years, Theo Papadopoulos and Audrey Lowe are reunited. We'll have their first public interview, together, right after these messages."

The spotlights faded as the show transitioned to commercial. The network's legal disclaimer played in quadruple speed over the title card.

"The Network of America does not condone or support any of the views or beliefs held by the guests of The Tonight Show with Jimmy Holiday. The safety of our sponsors and viewers is The Network of America's highest priority. It is important you understand our Community Guidelines, and the role they play in our shared responsibility to keep our society safe. You can read our policy by following us on social media and subscribing to our video channels, where you can play fun games like Purple Diamond Hunter!"

Theo didn't hear any of that. He only had ears for Audrey.

"I'm sorry, Theo," she whispered into his ear. "I'm so sorry."

CHAPTER 5: DON'T YOU (FORGET ABOUT ME?): BRAIN TRAUMA AND ITS EFFECTS ON MEMORY

BEFORE "THEN"

"Prove it," said Benny. He sat with his arms folded underneath the seat belt.

"It goes this far, right?" Theo tugged on his seat belt. The *ka-thunk* of the mechanism stopped him, pulling six inches from his chest. "It only lets you go so far. That's why you should have your arms outside it. Any extra slack means it's more dangerous. You'll fly forward more, and your brains will scramble."

Benny laughed. "Brains don't scramble."

"Can. Yours already is." Theo went for the ticklish spot on Benny's neck. He began to convulse back and forth in breathless delight. "Look, it's all mush."

Benny could barely cry through his laughter. "Stop it!"

"If your brain isn't mush, what's eight times eight?"

"I …" (Laugh.) "… fifty something." (Laugh.) "I can't think!"

"It's sixty-eight," said their dad from the driver's seat. His attention was fixed on the road when they were in the car. Their father's inability to focus on more than one thing at a time was a rich well of family amusement.

"No, it's not," said Theo, starting to laugh himself.

"Sixty-six?" Their dad's Greek accent became more pronounced the more confused he got.

Theo and Benny doubled over in the back seat they were laughing so hard.

"Dad, you should know this!" said Benny, almost hyperventilating.

"It's definitely in the sixties ..."

"Race!" declared Theo. He shifted to look at Benny. "Come on, Benny. You're smarter than Dad."

Benny giggled, and then his face fell into a deep concentration. Theo knew Benny hadn't started his eight times table yet; that's why he brought it up. Personally, he found eights the most difficult. Where other numbers lined up neatly, eight was too curved to get a grip on. Theo never really learned his eight times table. He just learned the answers, able to pass his test through repeating what adults had told him rather than developing a deeper understanding of how the number eight worked, and multiplied and stacked them on top of each other like a never-ending tower of fallen infinity loops.

Theo did understand one thing, though: Benny could work out problems like this instinctively. He saw numbers like they were stories. Theo admired that deeply. He wanted to help Benny be the best he possibly could be. He loved Benny.

"Sixty-four," Benny said, a fraction of a second after he was asked.

"*Skatá*. I knew it was in the sixties," said their father, his eyes never leaving the road.

Theo squeezed Benny's hand in his own. Benny beamed at his older brother's approval.

"The problem is," said their dad, "I've got too much information in my head. It's all full up. The eight times table must've been pushed out somewhere."

This set the brothers off in another fit of laughter.

"That's not how it—"

Benny was cut dead by the world through the window streaking madly into a spinning blur, an aching, bruising, vomiting blur where nothing made a sound until it did, and red dots

and red dots

and red dots

blinked everywhere.

Audrey held his face between her hands. Her palms were icy on his cheeks.

"You were in a car accident. The one that killed Benny. You were in the car."

"It's so amazing to see you, Audrey. All this time, I've been trying to fight for your work."

Audrey clenched her eyes. "Listen to me, really *try* to listen to me. Look at my mouth as I tell you this."

"I'm listening," said Theo, focusing so intently he could see the creases in her lips.

"You suffered a serious brain injury. That is why you were targeted for the experiment. I was studying dissociative states and their links to head trauma. You never spoke to your dead brother. It was all in your mind. Your defective mind."

Theo nodded. "I'm going to show them how it works."

He saw her lips begin to tremble. "You can't hear me, can you?"

Theo squeezed her hand in his. "I can always hear you."

The crowd roared in delirious delight through the commercial break. People would whoop and cheer at random, close intervals, unprompted by the dimmed red applause light above the stage. Jimmy Holiday kept muttering under his breath, "What a moment" as a makeup artist touched up his face.

"Please, *please*, don't show them. They won't understand. This has all gone too far."

"I need to show them. This is what we set out to do together. To save the world."

"Oh, Theo," Audrey said. Her hair was still auburn brown, but the roots had turned gray. "I was wrong."

Theo rested a hand on her shoulder. Her cardigan felt soft in his palm. "Now I can give you everything you deserve."

"The experiment was flawed, Theo. I got drained by it. I got drained by you and your stories. I wasn't in a good place at the time. I've not been in a good place for a very long time."

But her voice was lost in the studio applause. Red dots above camera lenses encircled them.

"Welcome back …!"

"… you bastard!" Audrey screamed, yanking on the door handle. It made the car rock from side to side.

Stephen sat inside, his eyes fixed ahead. He spoke, but the window muffled his voice.

"I can't hear you, dickhead!" she shouted.

He lowered the automatic window a centimeter.

"I was saying you are causing a scene."

Audrey screamed a guttural, obscene howl. She *was* causing a scene. She had gone straight to Stephen's school after meeting with Terrance Kettering. Her hand was wrapped in toilet roll and dripping with blood. He ran away from her through the playground and locked himself in his car. Teachers and students had gathered by the building entrance to watch.

"You ruined it! *Royal Scientific*, gone. Talks, canceled. Book publishers dropped me. You've ruined *everything!*"

"I've only got an hour for lunch, Audrey. Please move out the way of the car so I can drive to the sandwich shop."

She kicked the car. "The sandwich shop is only a ten-minute walk away." She kicked it again. "It probably takes longer to drive."

"You do know this is your car too. There's no point kicking yourself."

"Get out of the car, Stephen."

"I don't want to. You're being dramatic."

"I'm being dramatic?" she said very dramatically. "You have just gone behind my back and sabotaged my career. If there is any drama here, it's because you caused it. *You* are to blame."

"Classic Audrey," he said, still not looking at her. Kids had started laughing and doing impressions of her. "You criticize everyone else for not listening to each other. You even try to medically diagnose them for not listening to each other. And yet I don't think you've ever tried listening to yourself."

Audrey wrenched the handle again. Kicked the car again.

"Have you ever thought that you might be to blame?" said Stephen. "That maybe it is all your fault? That *you* really did exploit that poor, grieving kid, and that it *was* you who screwed up your career?

"You should be thanking me, Audrey. Because it would've come out sooner or later. And that would've been even worse."

Audrey pressed her face up against the window gap.

"I would be thanking you, Stephen, if you fucking told me *before* you went right to the editor of the *Royal Scientific!*"

"Maybe I did," he said. He finally turned to face her, his eyes bloodshot through the window. "And maybe you just didn't listen."

"... to *The Tonight Show with Jimmy Holiday*, that's me, where I'm joined by two very special guests, reunited for the first time in over a decade, the Living Proof Theo Papadopoulos, and the scientist whose work he's been fighting to restore for ten whole years, the hopefully soon-to-be Dr. Audrey Lowe!"

Jimmy Holiday leaned over to Theo. "What do you think of that? Living Proof, as a nickname? I just came up with it."

"I could tell." Theo smiled. The crowd delighted in the banter.

Jimmy Holiday feigned hurt. "We'll get into your amazing story together, but first, before the break, you have something to unveil to the world. Theo, ladies and gentlemen, is going to reveal how he talks to other dimensions!"

Theo could feel Audrey's eyes on him, pleading, willing him on.

"Don't," Audrey whispered behind her hand. "Please. Don't."

"We're all very excited to see this—a world exclusive!—so please, without further ado ..."

Jimmy Holiday bowed sitting down, ceremoniously passing the hosting duties to his guest.

Theo bent over to reach beneath his seat. His hand found the strap of a duffel bag. He pulled it out and hoisted it onto his lap. It was light. There was only one object inside. Audrey placed a hand on his wrist in encouragement. He looked in her eyes.

"*Don't.*"

He nodded and opened the bag. The studio was utterly quiet, heavy with anticipation. The zipper sounded like a tear through time and space in its silent void. Theo reached inside and carefully brought out a silk drawstring bag. It felt magically soft in his hands. The purple fabric had the iridescent glisten of a seashell in the overhead studio lights. He untied the drawstring and placed his hand into the bag. He stood.

"This is the secret to everything," Theo said. He pulled out the object of his power. In his hand, he held the humerus bone from his brother's skeleton. "This is my TeleBone."

The studio remained silent, but a different kind of silent. The air shifted with the ventilation system. Audrey put her head in her hands, trying to fold into herself like a dying multiverse.

Theo raised the TeleBone slightly higher.

Jimmy Holiday was staring at the object, his brows tight with confusion, stuck between asking out of curiosity and his default of trying to set up a joke.

"Erm, right. This is a, um. It's obviously a … thing. What exactly is it that we have here?"

"This is my TeleBone."

"Okay." Jimmy Holiday blinked, not for intended comic effect. "And what. What is a TeleBone?"

"This is the device I use to communicate with other dimensions."

"Right. And what, specifically, is the TeleBone? Because it looks a lot like—"

"A human bone."

"A human bone, yes. Right." Jimmy Holiday moved his sobering-up eyes from the bone to Theo, seeing him anew. "And you speak to your dead brother on that?"

"That's how I do it. That's why I call it a TeleBone."

"Like a telephone?"

"Yes."

"Right."

Audrey took hold of Theo's non-bone-holding hand. She was proud of him. That now her research could finally be recognized.

The crowd didn't start to boo. They made a different noise. They started to groan long, drawn-out groans. Far beyond the fake groans to Jimmy Holiday's intentionally bad one-liners. These were groans in anguish. Groans of realization that they'd been fooled by a fool.

A man stood up three rows from the front.

"You're a crackpot!" he heckled in a British accent. "Four years of my life, four years I followed you ..." He politely pushed people's knees aside as he stormed off out the aisle. "Wasted!" he shouted when he reached the stairs.

Theo turned back to Jimmy Holiday. He noticed the host's head had dropped, looking down at his shoes. He had never seen the great Jimmy Holiday so shocked. This must be going very well.

"It's a good gag," was all Jimmy Holiday could muster. "TeleBone ..." He chuckled. "It's a good gag."

The show cut to commercial.

Dont believe everything u see.

That was a LIE! That was NOT Theo.

Trust me ive known Theo for two years. Hes told me I'm his closest friend and the person who gets him more than anyone. We stay up every night talking about our discoveries and theories on how the world is put together just to benefit THEM.

Anyone who has lost faith, remember that. Remember THEM.

Theo Papadopoulos is a great man. weve let him into our lives night after night after night with his videos. In fact we've not just let him into our lives, weve GIVEN him our lives because we believe him.

And now just because of one show, people dont believe him.

i say to all of u traitors that are turning you r backs on us— LISTEN. Listen to what Theos been saying.

Questions everything.

PROVE yourself.

PROVE

PROOOVE

PROVE

What's more likely? That Theo doesnt actually talk to other dimensions (when we KNOW he does), OR the 10 men got their latest marching orders from the nafier PEDOS to SHUT HIM DOWN. When you lay it out like that, it speaks for itself. What more proof do you need when something is so obvious???

That Theo Papadopoulos on the Jimmy Holiday show

WAS.

A.

ROBOT.

He was a ROBOT created by the 10 MEN to DISCREDIT us.

Watch back the clip at 3.08. See how Theo doesn't seem to respond to the true Doctor Audrey Low? And DOCTOR Audrey Low keeps mouthing "don't" to him. Something IS NOT RIGHT HERE!!!

We must continue Theo's mission. I know the REAL Theo is still out there. We've got to find him.

Subscribe to my channel where im going to be doing a livestream every night on my search for the real Theo. We MUST keep his ideas alive.

PROVE YOURSELF,

PhilMeUpButtercup95

P.S. Im very sorry if theres any spelling mistakes or anything in this post. i broke my thumb recently in an accident and its still bandaged up.

NOW

Audrey and Theo sat beside each other on some cold metal stairs down an alleyway several blocks from the *Tonight Show* studio. She had raced him off as soon as their segment had ended. Theo assumed it was to protect him from the thousands and thousands of people, not to mention top-level military personnel, now likely in pursuit of his TeleBone. The thought of the army, who were really under Na'fier control, confiscating it made Theo shiver. Had he done the right thing, revealing it to the world? He felt Audrey's hand, still ice cold, grip his own, and he knew he had.

The December air was sharp and carried a whiff of pizza slices to the back road's smell of stale piss. Traffic angrily honked and backfired from the other end of the alley. They were a long, long way from home.

"Something's changed, hasn't it?" he said.

"Everybody knows now, but I bet nothing will change in the long run." Her breath fogged, each sentence coming out ghostly in the night's air. "Someone else will come along claiming to have all the questions and all the answers. People will subscribe. The world will keep turning."

"I meant … something has changed in me." Theo ran a hand through his long hair. It was itchy and heavy, and he felt an urge to cut it all off. "Before, I had a secret. But now I've showed everyone my TeleBone, I feel like emptiness has filled up the place where the secret used to be. Is there an answer for that in psychology?"

Audrey turned to him, her eyes puffy and red. "I'm so sorry, Theo. I used you."

"I was happy to be used. You deserve recognition for everything you've done."

"No, you're not hearing me. And you won't hear this either, I guess. The mics picked up what I said to you in the commercial break. One of the bastard producers posted it online. Everyone knows about your brain injury now."

"That's what we both wanted."

"That's what I wanted, Theo. You wanted something totally different. And you think you got it, don't you? You're so ignorant. It must be bliss. Not knowing what you don't know."

Theo smiled. "I might not know much, but I know you're a good person."

Audrey's eyes stung, and then became unbearably dry, and then she started crying, like a container behind her face had finally become full and overflowed. She thought of the heat in the car eight years ago. She thought of the sky breaking.

"I've done so much wrong, Theo. I should never have used you the way I did. I should never have used any of the subjects the way I did." She inhaled sharply, the subzero air stinging her lungs. "I should never have married Stephen. I should never have cheated on Stephen. I should never have let things get this big and out of control." Her breath peaked. "I should have just gone to see my grandad."

Theo gently patted her back until she calmed.

"I just want to see my grandad."

"I know," Theo said, his hand transitioning into slow, circular rubs. "I just want to see Benny."

They sat there for a time, in the December New York chill.

"You were the only one who ever listened to me, Audrey. My parents shut down after my brother died. I had nobody to talk to anymore. Whatever happens, whatever *happened*, I'll always love you for that."

He reached around with his other arm and gave her a brief, intense hug. For a moment, he was a teenage boy again. Isolated, ignored, delusional. Independent, inquisitive, hopeful.

Now she knew how that must have felt. She realized that's what she'd been feeling her entire life.

"You don't love me," she said. "You don't hear words. You just hear the gaps."

Theo pondered what she said, almost as though he'd actually heard her.

"The gaps are where the meaning is," he said.

Theo produced the TeleBone from his pocket. He held it in front of her. The moonlight gleamed off its pocked collagen, just how it had under the overhead studio rig. They looked up together. It was a full moon. Wide and awake and staring. The red light had finally turned white.

"You can talk to him if you want. Your grandad."

Audrey watched her hand float forward, caught in a tractor beam of moonlight, felt her fingers touch its dry surface. *Dry as a bone.* She lifted it up to her ear, the receiver end reaching down to her mouth.

She spoke. Theo listened.

ACKNOWLEDGEMENTS

Firstly, thank you Kiki, the best cat in the world. Meow meow meow meow, meow.

Secondly, thank you to the humans. My two writing dads, Zah and Chris (one is lovely and encouraging, the other makes you do 38 drafts of the same line. Both approaches are needed), and the E17 writing group of Lizzie, Giulia, Renan, the "G-Man" Geoff, Lois, Scott and other Ollie. Particularly Lizzie, who would write with me in cafes and pubs (depending on the time of day) and for being the first person to read a much earlier, far worse draft; and Chris, who both guided me through his torturous 38 draft approach, and for helping research publishers to approach. Without you all and your support, writing would've just stayed an idle dream in my head.

Thank you to Jessica, Amie and Melanie at Vine Leaves Press for taking a chance on me, even though I wrote a noncommercially viable novella.

Thank you to my conspiracy theory expert, for making sure I wasn't overlapping on any of the most definitely real ones.

Thank you to my mum, dad and sister, who have had no idea what I've been doing but were nurturing nonetheless. And to my nanny and grandad for loving each other for over seven decades.

And thank you to my partner and super teammate, Anna, who made a professionally bound and printed version of this story for me to keep my spirits up against rejections. Ultimately, I do everything just to impress you.

VINE LEAVES PRESS

Enjoyed this book?
Go to *vineleavespress.com* to find more.
Subscribe to our newsletter: